Kissed at Christmas Cottage

Rebecca Lange

Published by Rebecca Lange, 2022.

KISSED AT CHRISTMAS COTTAGE

First edition. November 21, 2022.

Copyright © 2022 Rebecca Lange.

ISBN: 978-1957089201

Written by Rebecca Lange.

Table of Contents

For those of you who love Christmas as much as I do...

May the snow fight dirty, snowblowers surrender in defeat, shovels mysteriously vanish, and the pastries be so good no one even pretends to feel guilty. You're welcome.

KISSED AT CHRISTMAS COTTAGE

First edition. November 21, 2022.

Second Edition. December 2025

1

A Love Unreturned

Ophelia hurried from the ballroom, her silk skirts whispering furiously against the marble floor. She would not stay another moment. And she most certainly would not court, let alone marry, the man her father had chosen for her. Another argument loomed on the horizon like an approaching storm, but for once, she found she did not care.

Before she could reach the front door, Lady Caroline Williams caught up and grasped her arm.

"Ophelia, wait! What are you doing?" Caroline's breath came quickly. Her cheeks flushed with alarm. "Why would you deny Lord Ainsworth the chance to court you? He is a decent and respectable baron, and—"

"Yes, he is decent," Ophelia cut in, her voice trembling with restrained defiance. "But I wish to choose my suitors. I want to marry for love. Is that truly so wrong?"

Caroline's expression softened with pity.

"No, of course not. But you never even give these young men a chance. Perhaps, with time—"

"My feelings will not change."

"This is the third suitor you've turned away," Caroline pressed. "You must think about the consequences. The Earl of Wyndham has already begun spreading unkind rumors because you refused to dance with him at the last ball. He's been quite persistent, as you know, and others may soon listen to his gossip and withdraw their interest."

Ophelia turned toward the window, the pale light outlining her slender frame. Her reflection in the glass looked back at her, stubborn, proud, and determined. She knew Caroline meant well, yet her friend's warnings only steeled her resolve.

"You know I've never cared for Lord Dalton's opinion," she said coldly. "He fancies himself a gentleman, but I am not deceived. He's a rake at best, and twice now, he's attempted to compromise me. I'll not let him, or anyone, destroy my reputation. My father may be disappointed, but I feel no guilt."

Caroline sighed. "This obstinacy of yours will hurt you one day. I could understand if these men were cruel or vulgar, but each has been respectable, and, truth be told, rather handsome." Her tone grew weary. "Your father tolerates your stubbornness for now, but eventually he may grow tired of it and force your hand."

Ophelia turned sharply, her blue eyes blazing.

"So, you expect me to marry merely to please my father?"

"That isn't what I'm saying," Caroline replied quickly. "I only think you might be acting rashly."

Ophelia crossed her arms. "Tell me, Caroline, would you marry Lord Camden if you didn't love him?"

Her friend hesitated. The confident poise of Lady Caroline faltered.

"It was my father's dearest wish that I would marry James Camden," she admitted.

"But would you have done so if your heart hadn't inclined that way?"

Caroline looked away. "I... honestly don't know."

"And do you believe your father would have forced you into such a match?" Ophelia pressed gently. Caroline's voice softened.

"No. My father did not believe in forcing anyone to do what their heart rejected."

"Then why," Ophelia asked, her tone quiet but cutting, "do you urge my father to push me into something I don't want? Why do you chastise me every time I refuse a suitor?"

Caroline's lips parted, but no words came. Her eyes dropped to the carpet. After a long silence, she took Ophelia's hand.

"Forgive me," she murmured. "You're right. I've been harsh. Your father only asked me to help you see reason, but believe me, both of us want nothing more than your happiness."

Ophelia's expression softened.

"I know you mean well, Caroline. But I cannot be happy with these men." Her voice trembled as she added, "My heart already belongs to one man."

Caroline's breath caught. Her gaze flickered with dread.

"Please, Ophelia... don't."

Ophelia smiled faintly, her eyes bright with memory.

"You know it's true. I've loved him for years."

Caroline's composure wavered. "You and my brother have always been dear friends, but—"

"But?"

"But he doesn't see you in that way."

The words struck like a physical blow. Ophelia's heart clenched, but she refused to surrender her hope.

"Perhaps, in time—"

Caroline shook her head. "No, my dear. You are like a sister to him. He cherishes you deeply, but not as a man cherishes the woman he loves."

"You cannot know that," Ophelia whispered. "People change. Feelings change."

Caroline hesitated, then gave a quiet sigh and squeezed her friend's hand.

"I wasn't supposed to tell you yet, but you deserve the truth. Oliver is recently engaged to Lady Isadora Phillips."

For a moment, the world went utterly still. Ophelia's breath caught, her pulse hammering in her ears.

"When?" she managed to whisper.

"Saturday last." Caroline's eyes searched her face, bracing for tears. "They've been courting through the summer. That is why my brother has been traveling to London so often. They plan to marry in the spring, and Lady Isadora will come to live at the estate."

Ophelia's vision blurred. She felt the floor tilt beneath her, as if the air itself had been drawn away. Caroline guided her to a chair, but Ophelia barely felt it. Her chest ached so fiercely she could hardly breathe. The man she had secretly loved, dreamed of, prayed for, was promised to another. After a long silence, Ophelia rose unsteadily to her feet.

"I need to be alone," she said, her voice trembling but dignified. "Please... excuse me."

"Ophelia—" Caroline began, reaching for her hand. But Ophelia stepped back. Without another word, she turned and fled the room. The door closed behind her with a soft thud, leaving Caroline standing in heavy silence. And in the corridor beyond, Ophelia pressed a hand to her chest as though to hold the shattered pieces of her heart together, yet even that, she feared, might not be enough.

Oliver Williams stepped out of the ballroom only moments after Ophelia had fled. The distant hum of the orchestra faded behind him, replaced by the faint rustle of silk gowns and murmured conversation from the adjoining corridor. His eyes immediately found his sister standing near the tall window, a troubled expression clouding her usually composed features.

"Caroline?" he asked quietly as he approached. "Are you well? You look distressed." His gaze flicked over her shoulder. "And where is Ophelia? I thought she was with you."

Caroline released a weary sigh and turned toward him.

"She was. But she's gone now. I told her—" She hesitated, wringing her gloved hands. "I told her about your engagement to Lady Isadora."

Oliver's brow furrowed. "Why? I thought we agreed to keep it silent for now."

"I had to," Caroline said gently, her voice tinged with regret. "She deserved to hear it from us before society made it public. It would have been cruel, to let her discover it through whispers and gossip."

For a long moment, Oliver said nothing. His gaze drifted past his sister to the empty hall, where the faint echo of Ophelia's hurried footsteps still seemed to linger. At last, he nodded slowly.

"You were right to tell her." His tone was quiet, thoughtful. "It was inevitable that she would learn the truth. I only wish it hadn't wounded her so deeply."

"She loves you, Oliver," Caroline said softly, her eyes full of compassion. "You must know that."

He exhaled, his shoulders, heavy.

"I do. I've known for some time. I had hoped, foolishly, perhaps, that she would eventually outgrow it, that she'd meet someone who could love her as she deserves." He paused, the faintest ache in his voice. "She is dear to me, one of the truest hearts I've ever known, but not in the way she wishes."

Caroline studied her brother's face, reading the quiet sorrow beneath his calm demeanor.

"You care for her deeply," she said. "I can see that."

"I do," he admitted, glancing toward the ballroom doors, where laughter and music spilled faintly into the corridor. "She has been part of our family since we were children. I never imagined that my affection for her, my friendship, might become a source of pain."

Caroline's expression softened.

"Then perhaps you should speak with her. She may not listen at first, but she deserves to hear your heart plainly. It might help her begin to heal."

Oliver nodded slowly, though uncertainty flickered in his eyes.

"Perhaps. Though I fear any words I speak tonight will only deepen her hurt."

"Still," Caroline murmured, touching his arm, "better honesty than silence."

Oliver looked down the corridor once more, where lamplight cast long shadows across the polished floor. Somewhere beyond those doors, Ophelia was nursing a broken heart, a heart he had never meant to wound.

"I'll find her," he said at last, his voice low with resolve. "She deserves at least that much from me." And with that, he turned away, his steps echoing softly as he went in search of the woman whose love he could not return.

As soon as Ophelia stepped out of the house, she gathered the hem of her gown above her ankles and ran, heedless of the chill that nipped at her cheeks. The night air was sharp, filled with the promise of snow, though autumn had not yet surrendered to winter. Her breath came in soft, visible clouds, but she did not slow her pace until she reached the back garden. She wanted to be alone. She needed to be.

The world around her seemed unnatural still, the branches bare and skeletal, the hedges frosted with the first hint of ice. Somewhere in the distance, the faint strains of the orchestra drifted from the ballroom windows, cruelly mocking her pain with their cheerful melody. She wrapped her arms around herself, shivering, not entirely from the cold, and glanced about for a place to hide. Then she saw it: the old treehouse, half-hidden among the towering oaks at the far edge of the garden.

A fragile smile flickered across her tear-streaked face. Her father had built it for her when she was a child, its wooden planks once painted a cheerful shade of blue. Time and weather had worn the color away, and the ladder creaked with age, but the little house still stood strong. It had always been her refuge, her secret haven from the world.

Lifting her skirts again, she hurried across the frosted grass and grasped the ladder's sides. The wood was cold and rough beneath her gloved hands as she climbed. When she reached the small landing, she opened the door and ducked inside, her breath trembling. It was as she remembered, dusty, small, but comfortingly familiar. The single wide window still overlooked the garden and the meadow beyond, its glass fogging with her breath as she leaned close. She sank down onto the worn wooden floor and buried her face in her hands.

Memories crowded in, the laughter she and Caroline had shared there on summer days, the sound of Oliver's voice as he joined them, teasing and good-natured. He had always been kind to her, even when she was a willful child demanding his attention. Somewhere between those sunlit afternoons and the evening he returned from London, everything had changed. Her heart had changed.

Oliver had taken it quietly, unknowingly. She had tried to tell herself that her feelings were foolish, that he saw her only as a friend, perhaps even as a sister. But whenever he looked at her with those gentle eyes, whenever he spoke her name with that familiar warmth, hope rose unbidden in her heart.

She pressed a trembling hand against her lips, trying to stifle a sob. He had returned from London a man, confident, capable, burdened by the title and responsibilities of his late father's earldom. The years apart had only deepened her admiration for him, and though she had tried to hide her love, Oliver had always been far too perceptive. He saw more than she ever wished him to.

But if he had noticed her feelings, he had never acknowledged them. He still treated her as he always had, with affection, with respect, but never with the tenderness she longed for. And now... now that tenderness belonged to another.

Ophelia pressed her forehead to the cold windowpane, her tears falling freely. Outside, a few snowflakes began to drift down, silent and delicate, settling against the glass. Her heart felt as though it had splintered into pieces too sharp to ever fit together again. She had given her love wholly, unquestioningly, and now she knew it would never be returned.

"I shall never love another," she whispered into the empty room, her voice breaking. "Not as I love him."

The wind sighed through the cracks in the wood, and the treehouse creaked softly, as if echoing her grief. There, in the small haven that had once been a place of childhood dreams, Ophelia wept, for the future she would never have, and for the man who would never be hers.

Oliver stood beneath the bare branches of the old oak, his breath clouding in the chill night air. Above him, through the soft fall of snow, he could hear it, the fragile, broken sound of Ophelia's sobs drifting from the little treehouse. The sound pierced him like a blade. He closed his eyes for a moment, his chest tightening. He had known this would wound her. Still, hearing her cry made the guilt settle heavier upon his heart. Ophelia was one of the brightest, most spirited souls he had ever known. That he had been the cause of her pain was something he would never forget.

She'll heal, he told himself quietly. *She must.*

Her hurt was deep now, but she was strong, stubbornly so. That fierce will, the very quality that so often exasperated her father, would carry her through this heartbreak as it had carried her through every other hardship life had placed in her path. She was a fighter.

He placed a gloved hand on the rough wood of the ladder and began to climb. Each creak of the old rungs sounded louder than it should have in the garden's stillness. As he reached the top, the sobbing ceased. He paused, listening. He could hear the faint rustle of fabric, the subtle sound of movement, she was turning away, likely facing the window so she would not have to look at him. Oliver drew in a slow breath and crouched to enter the small doorway.

The air inside was cool and faintly scented with the dust of old memories. Dim moonlight filtered through the window, illuminating Ophelia's slender figure as she sat with her back to him, her shoulders trembling despite her effort to remain composed. He settled beside her, leaving a respectful distance between them. For a moment, neither spoke. Only the whisper of wind through the trees filled the silence.

"Forgive me," he said softly, his voice weighted with sincerity. "Forgive me for failing you, Ophelia. I wish I could love you as you wish me to, but my heart belongs to someone else."

She did not look at him, but in the faint light, he saw her nod, a small, tight movement of acknowledgment.

"Would you like to talk about it?" he asked gently. Her reply came after a long pause, quiet and hoarse from tears.

"There's nothing to talk about. This is something I must come to terms with on my own."

He nodded slowly, though the words hurt him.

"If I ever made you believe there could be more than friendship between us, I am truly sorry."

"You didn't," she whispered. "You did nothing wrong. I only hoped..." Her voice faltered, the rest of the sentence lost to the night. Oliver waited, but when she did not continue, he knew she had said all she could bear. "Please," she murmured at last, "leave me be. I need time... time to think."

He looked at her for a long moment, the girl who had been his companion in childhood games, his confidante, his constant shadow. Her face was turned toward the window, pale in the moonlight, her eyes fixed on something far beyond his reach. With quiet reverence, he took her hand and gave it a gentle squeeze.

"You'll always have a special place in my heart, Ophelia," he said softly. "I can't give you what you desire, but I will always care for you, as a dear and cherished friend." He released her hand and rose. The low ceiling forced him to duck as he stepped toward the narrow doorway. For a moment, he hesitated, glancing back at her one last time. Then, with a heavy heart, he descended the ladder, his boots crunching faintly on the frozen ground below.

Oliver paused at the base of the tree and looked up at the little window glowing softly in the moonlight. Then he turned and walked back toward the estate, the white flakes settling silently upon his dark coat and hair.

Ophelia lifted her head only after the sound of his footsteps had faded completely into the night. For a moment, her tears had ceased, leaving her hollow and aching, but then they returned, hot and unrestrained, spilling down her cheeks as the weight of his absence settled fully upon her heart. She dragged herself closer to the window on trembling knees and pushed open the small wooden door. The cold air rushed in at once, sharp and unforgiving, biting at her cheeks and stinging her tear-dampened skin. She barely noticed. Below, in the dim glow of moonlight, she saw him crossing the garden, his tall figure outlined against the silver frost, his steps steady and unhurried, as though nothing within him had broken at all. Her throat tightened painfully, the ache so fierce it nearly stole her breath.

"I may have a special place in your heart," she whispered into the empty night, her voice trembling with quiet despair, "but not the place I want."

The wind carried her words away, scattering them into the darkness, unanswered. She closed the little door and sank back against the wall, her shoulders shaking as her tears fell freely once more. Outside, the snow continued to fall, soft, relentless, and silent, blanketing the garden below like a shroud laid gently over a love that had never been spoken aloud, and could never be returned.

2

The Name Beneath the Lies

The days that followed passed in muted stillness. Ophelia kept to herself, wandering the halls of Hethersett Manor like a pale shadow of the lively young woman she had once been. The servants, long accustomed to her cheerful laughter, now whispered softly when she passed, as though afraid their voices might startle her fragile calm.

Henry watched it all with quiet anguish. He had tried, on more than one occasion, to speak with her about her latest refusal of courtship, but his efforts met only with polite silence. It was as though his words struck against an unseen wall. She answered him civilly, yet her eyes remained distant, her thoughts clearly elsewhere.

He wasn't angry. Not this time. There was too much sorrow in her expression, too much of the lost, wounded look of a heart broken beyond mending. He suspected it had little to do with Lord Ainsworth's rejection and everything to do with something she could not bring herself to tell him.

At breakfast, he studied her quietly across the long table. Morning light streamed through the tall windows, glinting off polished silver, but it did nothing to brighten his daughter's face.

Her spoon stirred her tea absently; she hadn't eaten more than a few bites in days. Henry sighed.

If only I didn't have to leave her now. But duty called, and his affairs in London could no longer be postponed. The merchants, the banker, everyone, expected payment, and he was already behind. His reputation in Norwich was fraying. Whispers of the Viscount's debts had begun to circle like vultures. The once-proud name of Hethersett carried less respect with each passing month.

He rubbed his temples, the weight of it all pressing down like a physical ache. If only Clarice were still alive. Even now, years after her passing, his thoughts turned inevitably to her, the beautiful, willful woman who had dazzled London with her charm and bankrupted him with her appetites. She had adored the Season: the glitter of new gowns, the admiration of every eye. He had loved her for it, even as it ruined him.

His gaze drifted to the empty seat where she used to sit, and he pushed away his untouched plate. When his butler entered, with the morning post, Henry accepted the stack of letters with little interest, until he saw the seal. His brother's. He frowned. He was due to meet Richard in London later that week. For a letter to arrive now could only mean unpleasant news.

Henry rose and excused himself from the table, though Ophelia had already slipped away in silence, leaving her tea untouched. Inside his study, he broke the seal and unfolded the parchment. His eyes scanned the page quickly, his brow furrowing as he read. The contents made his stomach sink. There were hints of family matters that could not be delayed, talk of obligations, perhaps even another demand for money.

"Nothing in my life is ever simple," he muttered, letting the letter fall onto his desk. His gaze lifted to the portrait above the fireplace. Clarice smiled down at him, radiant and untroubled, her painted eyes glimmering with the same mischief that had once captivated him. He leaned back in his chair and exhaled heavily.

"Why did I love you so?" he whispered bitterly. "You left me with your debts, your dark secrets, and still, I miss you." For a long moment, he sat there, staring at her image. His thoughts turned to the letter she had left him before her death, the one that had revealed the truth she had hidden for so many years. That secret still haunted him, one more burden added to the long list of things he could never speak aloud. A sharp knock broke the silence.

"Enter," he called, straightening as his butler stepped into the room.

"Your carriage awaits, My Lord."

Henry nodded and gathered his papers, bills, and account notes from the desk. He hesitated only a moment longer, casting one final glance at the portrait. Then he reached for the folder filled with debts and documents and left the room. In the front hall, he paused.

"Has anyone seen Lady Ophelia?"

The housekeeper curtsied. "Not since breakfast, My Lord. She went for a walk, I believe."

Henry frowned faintly but said nothing more.

"Very well. Please bid her farewell in my stead and tell her I shall return within the fortnight."

"I certainly will, My Lord," the housekeeper replied. He nodded his thanks, then stepped outside. The carriage waited at the foot of the steps, the horses pawing at the frosted earth. He climbed in, settled his papers beside him, and glanced back once more at the manor, his crumbling estate, his grieving daughter, his ghosts.

A moment later, the driver snapped the reins, and the carriage rolled away, down the long, winding drive toward London, leaving behind a house heavy with silence and secrets.

By the time Ophelia returned from her ride, the sun had already begun to sink behind the distant hills, casting long shadows across the frosted grounds of Woodcrest Manor. Her cheeks were flushed from the cold, and strands of hair had escaped her bonnet to dance freely in the wind.

She knew her father disliked her venturing out alone, but she could not bear the company of anyone, not after the week she had endured. The solitude of the countryside, the rhythmic sound of hooves against the earth, and the occasional bark of the dogs that followed her were her only comfort.

Her father's four loyal hounds trotted faithfully beside her wherever she went, and though he would have scolded her for being reckless, she felt safe with them. Surely, they were protection enough. When she finally reached the stables, one of the stable boys hurried forward to assist her. He caught the reins as she dismounted and offered a respectful nod.

"Thank you, Thomas," she murmured softly before heading toward the house, her boots crunching over the thin layer of snow that had begun to settle. The thought of a hot bath and a quiet evening gave her the strength to keep moving. Her body ached from the ride, but her heart ached more deeply still.

As she stepped into the foyer, the warmth of the manor enveloped her. The scent of burning wood and polished oak filled the air. The housekeeper approached at once, dipping into a graceful curtsy.

"My Lady, his lordship has departed for London. He bade me extend his farewell to you."

Ophelia nodded faintly. "Thank you, Mrs. Parker."

The older woman hesitated, her eyes soft with concern.

"Will you be needing anything this evening, My Lady?"

Ophelia shook her head. "No, that will be all."

But as the housekeeper retreated, Ophelia's composure faltered. Her father was gone again, leaving the house heavy with silence. It should not have hurt, she knew his business affairs demanded it, but the emptiness that followed his departures always reopened old wounds. She missed her mother fiercely. Clarice Winter had been strict, unyielding, at times, but her love for Ophelia had never been in question. She had shielded her daughter from the excesses of London society, perhaps too much, but her heart had always been tender, beneath her firm exterior. Even now, years after her death, the house still seemed to echo with her mother's voice, her laughter, her scent.

Instead of going upstairs to summon her maid for a bath, Ophelia's feet carried her instinctively toward her father's study. There was comfort there, among his books and ledgers, where the scent of parchment and ink mingled with faint traces of his tobacco. She knew precisely where he kept the folder of her mother's letters, worn with age, tied with a pale blue ribbon. Whenever grief became too much to bear, Ophelia would read through those letters and feel, if only for a few moments, that her mother was near again.

Crossing the threshold, she shut the door quietly behind her and walked to her father's desk. The room was dim, lit only by the last gray light filtering through the curtains. She pulled open the drawer where the folder was kept, but instead of finding it immediately, her eyes caught on a letter lying loosely atop a pile of papers.

It was no longer sealed, the wax broken. Her uncle's handwriting was unmistakable, bold, precise, and slightly slanted. She hesitated. She was not in the habit of prying. But as her gaze swept over the first few lines, her breath caught. Her name was mentioned several times. Curiosity and unease warred within her.

Surely it cannot be anything of consequence, she told herself. Yet her pulse quickened as she drew out the letter and unfolded it. The opening paragraphs were mundane enough, formal greetings, remarks about her father's impending visit, but by the third paragraph, Ophelia felt her heart still within her chest.

> *Henry, something must be done. You can't keep this a secret any longer, or you must finally find a suitor for your daughter. I have received another letter from Clarice's sister in Scotland, threatening to contact the authorities if I continue to refuse to return the girl to her father. Clarice's sister does not yet know that it is you she should be looking for...*

Ophelia's eyes widened. *Return the girl to her father?* Her breath grew shallow as she read on, each line sinking like a stone into her stomach.

> *Clarice wrote to her sister after she took the child, but when her sister pressed her, she cut off all contact. The woman has been trying to find Clarice for years, hoping to bring her to her senses, but she is poor and cannot afford a thorough investigation... I fear she may have reached out to the duke himself...*

Her hands began to tremble.

You know me, Henry. I've kept your secret out of loyalty, but this is becoming dangerous. I know you were hoping to find a husband for your daughter to help with your debts, but with Ophelia refusing every suitor, you must now act quickly.

My dear wife has been gone for over a year, and I am seeking a new match. Considering your predicament, I would be willing to marry your daughter myself and provide the funds needed to save the estate. She might need to be persuaded, but in time she will understand. We are not related by blood, and this could be your chance to restore your fortune, and for me to produce an heir...

The letter slipped from her trembling fingers and landed on the desk. For several seconds, Ophelia could not move. Her heart pounded wildly, her breath coming in shallow gasps. Then, with a choked cry, she pushed back from the chair and covered her mouth, horror flooding through her.

"Marry him?" she whispered, her voice barely audible. "My own uncle?" Her stomach churned, and she gripped the edge of the desk to steady herself. The words *'produce an heir'* echoed in her mind until she thought she might be sick. But worse still, worse than the vile proposal, was the implication buried in the letter's opening lines.

Clarice took the child... return the girl to her father... She stared blankly ahead, her thoughts spinning. *Her father. Return the girl.* The words tangled in her mind, refusing to make sense. If Clarice had taken a child... then who was she?

Her gaze drifted to the portrait of her parents above the mantel. Henry's stern countenance and Clarice's elegant smile looked down upon her as they always had, but now, even the painting seemed to mock her with a truth she did not yet understand.

Could it be possible that Henry Winter was not her father at all? That the woman she had loved so dearly had taken her, from someone else? Tears filled her eyes as she pressed a trembling hand to her mouth.

"No... no, it cannot be true," she whispered, though even as she spoke, a terrible certainty was already forming in her heart. The room seemed to close in, around her, the air heavy and suffocating. She stumbled to her feet, staring down at the letter as if it might burst into flames beneath her gaze. One truth had already shattered her heart. Now another threatened to destroy her very sense of self.

Everything around Ophelia seemed to spin. The study swayed before her eyes, her pulse thundering in her ears, but she forced herself to breathe, to think. She had to find her mother's diary. If there were answers to the questions now tormenting her, they would be there. For several moments, she sat frozen, willing the dizziness to subside. Then, pushing herself to her feet, she hurried from her father's study and made her way down the corridor to her mother's old rooms.

The door creaked softly as she entered. Everything was exactly as her mother had left it, the rosewood desk, the faint scent of lavender lingering in the air, the lace curtains drawn halfway against the waning light. The sight of it struck like a knife to the heart. Memories crowded in. Her mother writing by lamplight, her gentle laughter, her firm but loving voice. Ophelia's eyes stung, but she blinked the tears away. She did not have time to grieve, not now. She needed the truth.

She began to search the desk. Drawer after drawer revealed nothing but correspondence, trinkets, and keepsakes. Then, as her fingers brushed along the inner panel of the desk, she felt a small ridge, an uneven seam. Her heart leapt. Pressing gently, she discovered a hidden compartment. Inside, nestled within the narrow space, lay a small, leather-bound diary. Her breath caught. Finally.

Ophelia drew it out with trembling hands and carried it to one of the armchairs near the window. She had barely opened the cover when a folded letter slipped free, fluttering to the carpet. Bending quickly to retrieve it, she froze at the sight of the familiar handwriting. It was addressed to her father. Heart pounding, she unfolded the pages.

Henry,

In case you don't return from London on time, I am writing this letter because there are things you must know. I have kept dark secrets from you, and I cannot leave this earth without confessing them. Please forgive me for everything I have done. I never meant to hurt you, or our daughter.

I am not Ophelia's mother. Ophelia is not even her real name. I was her nursemaid, and when her mother died, I tried to convince her father to marry me. He refused. In anger and despair, I took the baby and ran away. I met you

*not long after and told you I was a widow. That, too, was a
lie. I was never married.*

The words blurred before Ophelia's eyes. Her breath hitched as
she pressed a trembling hand to her mouth. Her mother, no, not
her mother, had stolen her? She read on, barely able to see through
the tears gathering in her eyes.

*Ophelia's real name is Mariah. She is the daughter of Lord
James Richard Kensington, the Duke of Kent.*

A strangled gasp tore from her lips. Her lungs constricted. The
Duke of Kent? Her real father? A man she had never met. Her
heart felt as though it had stopped altogether. The room tilted, and
for a moment she thought she might faint.

*I took Mariah's birth record and forged new documents
for us both as soon as I had the chance. I even invented a
deceased husband to make my story believable. At first, I
intended to blackmail the duke, but I grew so attached to
the child that I could not bring myself to do it.*

*I leave it to you, Henry, to decide what must be done.
Forgive me for placing such a burden upon you. I could not
face Ophelia, Mariah, with the truth myself. I know it will
devastate her, but she deserves to know her true father.*

*Lord Kensington is a good man. I acted out of bitterness
when he rejected me, but I know the pain he must have
endured, first losing his wife, and then his only child. I
regret what I did more than words can say.*

By now, Ophelia—*Mariah*—could no longer contain her tears. They spilled freely onto the parchment, blotting the ink. Anger, grief, disbelief, and a hollow ache of betrayal twisted within her like a violent storm. She forced herself to turn the final page, her gaze catching the last lines, written in a smaller, gentler hand.

> *If you decide to tell Mariah the truth, please share this next part with her. I want her to know that I have always loved her.*
>
> *Clarice*

Below that, written in a trembling hand, came the message meant for her.

> *My dearest girl,*
>
> *I know this truth will wound you deeply, and I do not deserve your forgiveness. But my love for you has always been real. I may not have given birth to you, but from the moment I first held you, you were my child in every way that mattered.*
>
> *I have made a terrible mess of many lives, and I must soon face my Creator with the weight of what I've done. Please believe that neither Henry nor your true father bears blame for my actions. The Duke of Kent lost his daughter because of me, and you lost your name, your heritage, but not my love.*

Remember this, my dear Mariah: family is more than blood. No matter what happens, you will remain in my heart, and in Henry's, forever.

Ophelia's—*Mariah's*—vision swam. She could not breathe. The sobs that tore from her chest were violent and raw, shaking her entire body. She pressed her fists to her mouth, trying to stifle the sound, but the pain refused to be silenced. Everything she had ever believed about herself, her family, her identity, her very name, had been stripped away in the span of a few unbearable minutes.

When at last she could stand no longer, she let the diary fall into her lap and bowed her head, weeping until her body ached. The air in the study grew stifling, heavy with the ghosts of secrets long kept. She needed air. She needed to escape. Stumbling to her feet, barely aware of the tears still streaking her cheeks, she fled the study, her steps quick and uneven down the hall. When she reached the front door, she flung it open with trembling hands and gasped for breath and nearly collided with two figures standing on the threshold.

3

A Cry at Dusk

"Ophelia?" Caroline cried, startled, reaching for her at once. "Whatever is the matter?"

Oliver was beside her in an instant, his expression sharpening with alarm as he took in Ophelia's ashen face and glassy eyes. Before she could form an answer, her vision blurred again, the world tilting violently around her. She clutched at her chest, fingers curling into the fabric of her riding habit as though she might anchor herself there.

"I can't—breathe," she gasped, each word torn from her in shallow, panicked gulps of air. "Please—let me go—I can't—" Her voice fractured into sobs. Her knees buckled beneath her before she could finish the thought.

"Ophelia!" Caroline shouted. Oliver caught her just in time, his arms closing firmly around her trembling form. Her body sagged against him, all strength gone, her head falling heavily against his shoulder as consciousness slipped away. He tightened his hold, lowering her carefully, his heart pounding as he searched her face.

"Ophelia, Ophelia, look at me," he urged, his voice both urgent and steady, fighting the fear that clawed at his chest. "You're safe. I've got you."

But her lashes fluttered once and then stilled. Her breath came faint and uneven, her body slack in his arms as the darkness claimed her.

Caroline knelt beside them, her hands trembling.

"Oh, Oliver, what has happened to her?"

Oliver did not answer at once. He gathered Ophelia closer, shielding her instinctively from the cold night air, his jaw clenched with dread as he looked down at the woman who lay unconscious in his arms. Whatever secret had driven her to such despair, he knew one thing with terrible certainty, it had nearly broken her. And he feared this was only the beginning.

Oliver wasted no time. With Ophelia unconscious in his arms, he carried her swiftly into the drawing room, his stride long and purposeful. Caroline hurried beside him, her skirts gathered in trembling hands, her face pale with alarm. He lowered the young woman gently onto a settee, arranging her carefully before brushing a few damp curls from her brow. Her skin felt chilled beneath his fingers, her breathing shallow and uneven.

"Ophelia," he murmured, leaning closer, searching her face for any sign of awareness. Within moments, hurried footsteps echoed in the corridor. Several maids appeared at the doorway, followed closely by the housekeeper and the steward, their expressions drawn tight with concern as they took in the sight before them.

"What has happened?" Mrs. Estelle Parker asked, her voice trembling as she pressed a hand to her chest. "Is she hurt?"

Caroline shook her head helplessly. "We don't know. She opened the door in tears. Said she couldn't breathe, and then she collapsed."

A maid hovered anxiously near the settee.

"Shall I fetch water, My Lady?"

"Yes, please," Caroline said quickly. "And a blanket."

"Should I send for the physician?" the steward asked, his brow furrowed. "Or perhaps send an express to her father in London at once?"

"Not yet," Caroline replied, though uncertainty flickered in her eyes as she glanced at her brother. "Let us wait a moment. She may have only fainted, from shock or exhaustion. She has been terribly overwrought these past days."

Oliver remained silent, his attention fixed entirely on Ophelia. He adjusted the cushions beneath her head and took her hand, his grip steady but gentle, as though willing her back through sheer determination.

The room filled with hushed movement, maids fetching water and blankets, the housekeeper murmuring instructions, the fire being stoked higher against the chill. Yet beneath it all, a heavy stillness lingered, thick with fear. Everyone waited, scarcely daring to breathe, as though the slightest sound might determine whether Ophelia would wake, or slip further away.

A soft moan broke the silence. Ophelia stirred, her lashes fluttering, open. At first her gaze was unfocused, then the faces surrounding her, came slowly into view, wide-eyed and full of pity. The pain in her chest flared anew. She tried to sit up, to hide her tears, but Oliver gently pressed a steadying hand to her shoulder.

"Don't move," he said softly. She looked at him, saw the fear and tenderness in his eyes, and her resolve crumbled. The tears came again, helpless, unrestrained. Without hesitation, Oliver gathered her in his arms, holding her close as her sobs broke through the stillness of the room.

No one spoke. The servants exchanged uncertain glances, unsure whether to stay or slip away quietly. Caroline's eyes glistened, but she held her composure, waiting for Ophelia's storm of grief to pass.

At last, when her breathing steadied and the worst of her sobs faded into trembling silence, Ophelia drew back. Embarrassed, she dabbed at her cheeks with a lace handkerchief and forced a fragile smile.

"Forgive me," she whispered hoarsely. "I didn't mean to alarm anyone. I'm... fine now."

Mrs. Parker stepped forward, her brows knitting together.

"Are you certain, My Lady? You gave us quite a fright."

Mariah nodded faintly. "I shall be well, Mrs. Parker. I am merely out of spirits."

The housekeeper hesitated, unconvinced, but finally inclined her head.

"Very well, My Lady. If you need anything, please ring."

When the door closed behind the retreating servants, the room fell into an uneasy silence, broken only by the low crackle of the fire. Caroline immediately reached for Mariah's hand, her grip warm and reassuring.

"Ophelia, dearest," she said softly, her brow creased with worry, "please tell us what's wrong. Did something happen to your father? Has there been an accident?"

Mariah shook her head, blinking back another surge of tears.

"No. My father is well. He left for London this morning."

"Then what has caused such distress?" Caroline pressed gently, though there was an urgency beneath her calm. "You frightened us terribly."

Mariah lowered her gaze, her fingers twisting in the folds of her gown. The truth burned on her tongue, heavy, volatile, impossible to ignore. It pressed against her chest, demanding release. She could not carry it alone. Not anymore. These two had always been her closest companions, her truest confidants, the ones who had shared her childhood, her laughter, her heartbreak. If there was anyone she could trust with the truth, it was them. She drew a long, trembling breath and lifted her eyes to meet theirs.

"There is something I must tell you," she said quietly, "something I only learned today."

Oliver stilled at once, his attention sharpening, while Caroline's hand tightened around hers.

"It concerns my mother," Mariah continued, her voice faltering. "And... who I truly am."

The silence deepened, heavy, with anticipation. And then, haltingly at first, then with growing urgency, Mariah began to tell them everything.

By the time she finished, the fire had burned low in the grate, casting flickering shadows across the stunned faces of Oliver and Caroline. Neither spoke for several seconds, too shaken to find their voices. Caroline was the first to recover. Her eyes were wide with disbelief, her voice trembling.

"You mean to tell us that Lady Clarice Winter, your mother, was not your mother at all? That she took you from the Duke of Kent?"

Mariah nodded, her voice barely above a whisper.

"It's all in her own handwriting. The diary and the letter... I read them myself."

Oliver leaned forward, his jaw tight, his fists clenched on his knees.

"And your father, Lord Winter, he knew?"

"It appears he did," she replied quietly. "The letter from my uncle confirms it. He has known since Lady Winter's death."

Caroline's expression hardened.

"And yet he chose to keep it from you. Worse, he intends to sell you into marriage to pay his debts? To your uncle, of all people?" Her voice rose with outrage. "That is unforgivable!"

"Caroline," Oliver warned gently, but his sister ignored him.

"No, I will not hold my tongue," she said fiercely. "You are no longer his responsibility, Ophelia—Mariah—and he should have confessed the truth the moment he learned it. To use you now as a means of saving his fortune? It is disgraceful."

Mariah lifted her gaze to meet her friend's fiery one.

"You are right to be angry," she said softly. "I am angry too. But I cannot forget that he raised me, that he gave me a home and a name when I had neither. For all his faults, Lord Winter has been kind to me."

"Kind?" Caroline exclaimed, incredulously. "He is attempting to barter you like property!"

Oliver exhaled sharply, his expression grave.

"It is not right," he admitted, "but desperation drives men to madness. The viscount stands on the edge of ruin. For a nobleman, one burdened with pride and debt, it must be intolerable."

Caroline turned on him, her eyes flashing.

"So, you mean to defend him now?"

"I am not defending his actions," Oliver replied evenly, though his tone was weary. "But I understand his reasoning. He fears disgrace, the loss of his title, and destitution. That does not excuse what he plans to do, but it explains it."

Caroline folded her arms, still bristling.

"You are far too forgiving."

Oliver glanced at Mariah, his expression softening.

"Forgiveness may not come easily," he said quietly, "but perhaps understanding will bring her peace. She's endured enough pain for one day."

Mariah's eyes shimmered with unshed tears as she looked between them, her oldest friends, now the only family she could trust.

"I don't know what I'm supposed to do," she whispered. "Everything I believed about myself is gone. Even my name..."

Caroline took her hand again.

"Then let us begin with the truth, dear one," she said gently. "You are Mariah Kensington, daughter of a duke. And whatever happens next, we shall face it together."

"Ophelia—" Caroline stopped herself mid-word, a faint blush coloring her cheeks. "I mean, Mariah," she corrected gently. "Forgive me, it will take some time to grow accustomed to calling you by your true name."

Mariah smiled faintly, though weariness still shadowed her eyes.

"I understand. I'm not sure I've yet grown used to it myself."

Caroline leaned forward, her expression earnest.

"How will you proceed from here? What will you do?"

Before Mariah could answer, Oliver interjected with a teasing grin.

"Perhaps we should simply continue calling you Ophelia. It might save everyone the confusion."

Mariah shot him a withering glance, though her lips twitched despite herself.

"Don't you dare, Oliver Williams," she warned. "As much as it unsettles me to have my entire identity upended, I am quite grateful that Ophelia isn't truly my name. I never liked it, it sounded too dramatic, too melancholy. I often wondered what the viscountess was thinking when she chose it."

Oliver chuckled quietly. "So, you've been living under protest all these years?"

"Entirely," Mariah replied, folding her arms. "I tolerated it out of respect for her, but truth be told, I always thought it a most peculiar choice."

Caroline laughed softly, then sobered once more.

"When is Lord Winter expected to return?"

"Within a fortnight," Mariah answered.

"And what do you intend to do before then?" Caroline asked. Mariah hesitated only a moment before her voice steadied with quiet determination.

"I wish to meet my father, my real father. I must see him with my own eyes, show him that I am alive, and let him decide whether he wishes to have me in his life."

Oliver leaned forward, his gaze steady and reassuring.

"He will not reject you, Mariah," he said firmly. "All of England knows the Duke of Kent's story, how his wife died and his infant daughter was stolen. He searched for years, hoping she still lived. After such loss, finding you would be the greatest joy imaginable."

Mariah blinked back fresh tears and looked at him with gratitude.

"You sound so certain."

"I am," Oliver said simply. "No man could endure such loss and not long for the chance to make it right."

Caroline tilted her head, studying her brother.

"Have you met the duke, then?"

"Not formally," Oliver replied. "But I have seen him in London on occasion, and during sessions of Parliament. He is well regarded, quiet, reserved, yet commanding. The sort of man who carries his grief with dignity."

Caroline turned back to Mariah.

"Do you suppose that explains why the viscountess never allowed you to go to London? She must have feared being recognized."

Mariah nodded thoughtfully. "Yes. I always wondered why she refused to let me attend the Season or be introduced to society. I believed it was overprotectiveness, but now... it all makes sense. She was terrified of crossing paths with him, or perhaps of him recognizing me."

Caroline frowned. "But she went to London herself quite frequently. How did she manage that without being discovered?"

"She was cautious," Mariah said quietly. "She never stayed long, and she always wore veils when traveling beyond Norwich. I thought it vanity, an eccentric fashion choice, but now I see it was fear. She adored shopping, of course, and spending money she did not have... but she must have lived every journey dreading discovery."

Caroline's expression softened. "It must have been a lonely way to live."

"It was," Mariah murmured. "For both of us, I think."

After a moment's silence, Caroline asked, "How will you arrange to meet your father? Will you write to him first?"

Mariah shook her head. "No. I doubt any letter would reach him safely. I can't risk the postmaster intercepting it, Mr. Jacobson must have followed Lord Winter's orders precisely. And even if it reached the duke, why should he believe a stranger's words? For years, women must have written to him, claiming to be his lost daughter. He would have no reason to trust me."

Oliver nodded gravely. "You're right. The duke has been deceived before, by impostors. He might not believe you at first, even with proof."

"That is why I must go to him in person," Mariah said firmly. "I must look him in the eye and show him the letters, the diary. Only then will he know the truth."

Oliver considered this, then said, "We must first discover where he currently resides. I can make inquiries through Lady Isadora's family. They have connections in Kent and London. I could send a telegram tonight and have an answer by morning."

Mariah's heart clenched painfully at the mention of Lady Isadora. She tried to smile, but it wavered.

"That would be very kind of you," she managed, though her voice trembled slightly. Oliver appeared not to notice her discomfort.

"If the duke is in London, you could accompany me when I leave in two weeks' time. Will he send word before leaving the city?"

Mariah nodded.

"Good. It will allow us to plan accordingly and help you arrive quietly, without crossing paths with Lord Winter or his brother."

Caroline raised a skeptical brow.

"And what then? She simply knocks upon the duke's door and announces herself?"

Mariah lifted her chin, determination shining through lingering tears.

"What choice do I have? I cannot wait until Lord Winter returns. I must try."

Caroline sighed. "And if he does not believe you?"

Mariah looked away. "Then I will decide what to do when that moment comes. Perhaps I shall return to Norwich... or perhaps I shall not."

Oliver exhaled, a note of impatience threading his voice.

"Let us not borrow trouble before it arrives. I am certain that once the duke sees you, everything else will fall into place."

Caroline glanced at her brother, unconvinced but unwilling to argue further.

"Very well," she said at last. "Once you receive word, let us gather again and make final arrangements. You and I will pack your trunks together, Mariah. And Oliver, send an express to Lady Isadora's family tonight. It may take time for a reply, and we must plan for delays."

Oliver gave a firm nod. "I'll see to it as soon as we return home."

As the siblings exchanged a look of quiet resolve, Mariah leaned back, her heart torn between fear and hope. In just a fortnight, she might come face-to-face with the man whose blood ran in her veins, a stranger, yet her father. For the first time since reading Clarice's confession, she felt the faintest flicker of hope take root within her.

Lord Winter sent word sooner than expected. He had been away only seven days when an express arrived, announcing that he would depart London the following day. Fortunately, Oliver and Caroline Williams and Mariah had been preparing diligently for her journey, anticipating the need for haste. Nearly everything was ready. Only her trunks remained to be packed.

That evening, as the pale light of dusk filtered through the drawing room windows, Oliver and Caroline met with Mariah to finalize the details of her departure. The air was thick with both anticipation and unease, for each of them knew that what lay ahead could alter Mariah's life forever.

As Mariah stood upon the threshold, watching her friends' carriage disappear down the long drive, a heaviness settled over her heart. The air was sharp with the scent of approaching frost, and the wan winter light stretched thin across the gardens. Soon she would leave this place, her home, her memories, and even Lord Winter himself.

Despite the pain his deception had caused, it would not be easy to go. This manor, for all its secrets, had been her world. She knew every echo in its halls, every creak of its stairways, every hidden place in the gardens where she once played. The thought of London, a city she had never seen, filled her with both dread and aching curiosity.

Her throat tightened as she reflected on all she had learned in the past seven days. It felt as though her entire life had been uprooted and cast into a storm. Though she knew the affection Lord Winter and his late wife had shown her had been genuine, the knowledge of their deception still cut deep. She pressed a trembling hand to her chest, as if to steady her aching heart. A gust of wind swept through the open doorway, sending a chill along her spine.

She stepped back, meaning to close the door and return to the drawing room, then froze. Somewhere beyond the gardens, faint and desperate, came a cry.

Mariah lifted her head, her brow furrowing. She held her breath and listened. For a moment, there was only the wind sighing through the trees, the rustle of dry leaves skittering across the gravel. Then it came again, clearer this time. A woman's voice, calling for help. Her pulse quickened. She stepped out onto the stone steps, straining to see. The wind tore loose strands of hair from her pins, golden curls whipping about her face as she scanned the front lawn and the long drive beyond.

A figure appeared in the distance, running, stumbling, skirts torn, hair disheveled. The woman's cries grew louder as she came closer, her eyes darting fearfully over her shoulder. Moments later, the thunder of hooves echoed from the same direction. Mariah's heart leapt into her throat. She hurried forward just as the young woman faltered, her legs giving way beneath her. Mariah caught her before she struck the ground. The girl was gasping for breath, trembling violently, tears streaking her dirt-smudged face.

"Help me, please!" the young woman cried, clutching Mariah's sleeves. Within moments, the steward and several footmen rushed from the house. Behind them came Mrs. Estelle Parker, the housekeeper, her face pale with alarm.

"What has happened?" Mrs. Parker demanded, kneeling beside Mariah to help steady the girl.

Mariah looked down at her, her voice calm but urgent.

"She's terrified, someone is chasing her."

The girl gulped for breath, struggling to speak through her sobs.

"My name is Martha Cox. I—I serve the Earl of Wyndham. Please, you must help me. I'm with child."

A collective gasp rippled through those gathered. Mrs. Parker's eyes widened.

"You're not married, are you, child?"

Martha shook her head, fresh tears spilling down her cheeks. Mariah's stomach turned cold, as she exchanged a grave glance with the housekeeper.

"Martha," she said gently, "who did this to you?"

The girl broke down completely, her shoulders shaking.

"It was the earl," she sobbed.

"Did he force himself upon you?"

Martha nodded, her voice barely audible. Mrs. Parker drew in a sharp breath.

"Good heavens. And has he—has he done this more than once?"

"Yes," Martha whispered. "I told him today that I was with child. He became enraged, struck me, and sent his men after me. I ran, but they're close behind. He swore he'd have me killed before letting me shame him."

The sound of pounding hooves grew louder.

"Mr. Grayson," Mariah said firmly, turning to the steward, "take her inside at once. Send for two maids and have them tend to her injuries. Make certain she is safe."

The steward bowed his head. "As you wish, My Lady." Without hesitation, he lifted Martha into his arms and carried her inside. Mariah turned back toward the drive just as two riders emerged from the shadows, grim-faced men clad in the Earl of Wyndham's livery. They reined in sharply and dismounted.

"Make way at once!" one of them barked. Mariah's eyes flashed.

"How dare you speak to me in such a tone?" she said coldly. "I am the daughter of Lord Winter, and you will remember yourself."

"The Earl of Wyndham has commanded us to retrieve his servant," the man replied stiffly. "You have no right to interfere."

"We have every right," Mariah shot back. "This is the estate of the Viscount of Hethersett. The earl holds no authority here."

The man took a step forward, but one of Lord Winter's footmen blocked his path. The steward returned at that moment, positioning himself at Mariah's side, his expression hard.

"I have my orders, My Lady," the earl's footman snarled. "The girl belongs to the earl, not you. Best stay out of this."

Mariah's temper flared. "Belongs to him?" she repeated incredulously. "She may be in his employ, but she is not his property. Does your master truly believe his rank grants him ownership, of another human being? He is a coward and a scoundrel who has already ruined that poor girl's life and now seeks to silence her to save himself from scandal."

The man's jaw tightened. "Whatever passed between the earl and the girl is no concern of yours."

"It is my concern," Mariah snapped. "This house will not turn away a woman in need. Now leave this property at once, or you will regret ever setting foot upon it."

The riders exchanged uneasy glances, clearly unaccustomed to such defiance. Mrs. Parker stepped forward, her voice calm but cutting.

"You heard Lady Winter," she said firmly. "The young woman is under our protection. If you do not leave immediately, I shall see to it that the dogs are released."

The men looked around. Four burly footmen stood ready, their expressions stony and unyielding. After a tense moment, the riders muttered under their breath, turned on their heels, and mounted their horses. Without another word, they rode off, disappearing into the deepening dusk.

Mariah remained on the steps, the cold wind tugging at her hair, her heart pounding fiercely. The weight of everything, her shattered identity, her uncertain future, and now this desperate stranger's suffering, pressed heavily upon her. She drew a steadying breath and turned to Mrs. Parker.

"See that Martha is made comfortable," she said quietly. "No harm will come to her while she remains under this roof."

"Yes, My Lady," the housekeeper replied, her voice soft with pride. "You did right, Lady Winter. You did very right."

As the last of the riders vanished down the road, Mariah gazed toward the darkened horizon, her jaw set. For the first time since learning the truth of her past, she felt something stir within her, stronger than despair. Something like purpose.

4

The Price of Defiance

Mariah moved swiftly down the servants' corridor, her skirts brushing against the narrow walls. The scent of soap and firewood hung in the air, mingling with the faint clatter of dishes from the kitchen beyond. Her sudden appearance caused a small commotion, maids and footmen alike sprang to their feet, bowing and curtsying in startled confusion. It was not every day that a lady of the house ventured into the servants' wing. Whispers rippled through the room as Mrs. Parker and Mr. Grayson followed close behind her.

"Please," Mariah said gently, lifting a hand. "Do not make yourselves uncomfortable. Carry on with your work. I am only here to check on Miss Cox." Her calm tone and warm smile did much to ease their unease, though curiosity still flickered in their eyes. Moving further into the room, she found Martha lying on a settee, a folded blanket draped over her trembling form. The young maid attempted to rise when she saw Mariah approach, but Mariah immediately reached out to stop her.

"No, please, stay where you are," she said softly. "You've been through enough for one day. You must rest."

Martha sank back, her cheeks flushing with embarrassment.

"We've already sent for a physician," Mariah continued. "He should arrive shortly. I only wished to see how you were faring. Are you in much pain?"

"A little, ma'am," Martha whispered. "But I'll be all right."

Mariah nodded and lowered herself gracefully onto the edge of a nearby chair.

"Tell me, do you have family close by?"

"My family lives in London, ma'am."

"Do they know of your... circumstances?"

Martha hesitated before nodding. "Yes. I wrote to my father after—after it happened."

"And what did he say?"

Tears welled in the girl's eyes. "He told me to come home at once. He said he didn't care what the earl had done, that I would always have a place with them. But... I have no means to get there."

Mariah's expression softened. "You've been very brave to come this far." She reached out and took Martha's hand. "I am to leave for London the day after tomorrow. If you wish, you may travel with me. I will see that you are reunited with your family."

Martha stared at her, wide-eyed.

"I couldn't possibly accept such generosity, My Lady. I have no money for the journey. My family is poor, they will take me in, but I must find work to help support them. There are six younger children, and—"

"Hush," Mariah interrupted kindly, giving her hand a reassuring squeeze. "I did not ask for money. You shall come with me as my maid for the journey, and when we reach London, I will see to it that you find honest work in a respectable household, one where no man will dare treat you cruelly again."

Martha's lower lip trembled. "You would do that... for me?"

"Of course," Mariah said with a small smile. "You deserve a chance to begin anew. And no woman should ever be punished for the sins of the man who wronged her."

The young maid burst into quiet tears, murmuring her thanks. Mariah rose, smoothing her skirts.

"Rest now," she said gently. "I will send word when the physician arrives." With one final encouraging look, she turned and left the room, Mrs. Parker and Mr. Grayson following close behind.

The moment they stepped into the corridor, Mrs. Parker spoke, her voice edged with concern.

"You're leaving for London, My Lady? Does Lord Winter know of this plan?"

Mr. Grayson glanced at her as well, his brows furrowed in quiet apprehension. Mariah paused, weighing how much to tell them. For years, she had trusted these two more than anyone else in the household. They had been part of her life since childhood, Mrs. Parker, the warm yet shrewd matron who had guided her through girlhood, and Mr. Grayson, the loyal steward who had managed her father's estate with unwavering integrity. They had earned her honesty.

"No," she said at last, her tone even. "He does not know. And I must ask that he not be informed, not until I am gone."

The housekeeper's eyes widened slightly.

"My Lady, forgive me for saying so, but this sounds dangerous. You have never traveled alone before."

"I will not be alone," Mariah replied. "Lord Oliver Williams will accompany me as far as London. Once there, I intend to seek out the Duke of Kent."

Both servants fell silent. Mariah looked between them and gave a faint, wry smile.

"You are not nearly as shocked as I expected. You already knew, didn't you?"

Mr. Grayson's gaze dropped briefly.

"We suspected, My Lady," he admitted quietly. "We knew you were not the viscount's true daughter, though we did not know the full truth. We had heard the rumors of His Grace's missing child, of course, and I often wondered, but only now, hearing the duke's name spoken aloud, does the answer seem unavoidable."

Mrs. Parker shook her head in disbelief.

"To think the late viscountess would steal a child, and from a duke, no less. It is unspeakable."

Mariah folded her hands before her.

"Yes. It is horrifying. But you can understand why I must make this journey. If I wait for Lord Winter's return, he may try to prevent me. I do not wish to give the Duke of Kent any reason to condemn him, or to see him imprisoned for what has already been done. Perhaps if I go myself, I can soften whatever judgment may follow."

Mr. Grayson inclined his head solemnly.

"A wise decision, My Lady. And a brave one."

Mrs. Parker reached out and patted Mariah's gloved hand.

"You have our word. Your secret will remain safe. No one in this house will hear a whisper from us."

Mariah smiled faintly, her eyes glistening.

"Thank you, Mrs. Parker. You have both been so good to me."

"What will you tell Lord Winter?" the steward asked gently.

"I will leave him a letter," Mariah said after a moment's pause. "He deserves at least that much. I will explain what I have learned and why I must go. Perhaps, in time, he will understand."

Mrs. Parker gave a small nod. "If anyone can mend what has been broken, My Lady, it is you."

Mariah drew in a steady breath, glancing toward the passage that led back to the main wing of the house.

"I only hope," she murmured, "that my true father is the man the late viscountess described, and that he will want to know me." With that, she lifted her chin, squared her shoulders, and walked toward the fading light at the end of the corridor, no longer simply the viscount's daughter, but Mariah Kensington, standing on the brink of reclaiming her rightful life.

"How will you reach London, My Lady?" Mr. Grayson asked, his brow furrowed with concern. Mrs. Parker stood beside him, equally attentive.

"Lord Williams has kindly offered me a seat in his carriage," Mariah replied. "Which makes Martha's arrival even more opportune. With her accompanying me, I shall not be traveling alone with the earl." She gave a playful wink, and both servants smiled despite their lingering worry. Mr. Grayson's expression sobered at once.

"And what shall we do if the Earl of Wyndham returns tomorrow in search of his maid?"

"Lady Caroline will join me in the morning to help pack my trunks," Mariah explained, "and I believe Lord Williams intends to call as well. Should Lord Dalton arrive before the Earl of Norwich returns, I will deal with him myself. But if he becomes aggressive, you are to send for Lord Williams at once. He will not hesitate to intervene. And as you know, Lady Caroline is engaged to the Marquess of Pedham, he would never allow anyone to threaten her or her friends."

Mr. Grayson nodded firmly.

"Very well, My Lady. I shall ensure that as many footmen as possible are on hand."

"So, the Earl of Wyndham truly mistreats his servants?" Caroline asked the following morning, her tone a mixture of disbelief and outrage. Mariah nodded solemnly.

"I'm afraid so. I suspected something unsavory about him the moment we met, but I never imagined he was capable of such cruelty."

"How could he?" Caroline demanded, her expression fierce. "To violate a maid and then strike her for the consequence, it's monstrous."

"Men like Lord Dalton," Mariah said quietly, "never believe they're to blame. They twist every sin into the victim's fault. And when confronted, they lash out, desperate to protect their pride."

Caroline's lips tightened. "He's a scoundrel."

"He's a swine," Mariah said flatly. That earned a small, grim smile from Caroline. "It is appalling," Mariah continued, her voice trembling with conviction, "that servants, and women in general, are offered so little protection. Men of power use their rank as a shield for every wicked act, and the world turns a blind eye."

Caroline nodded. "You were brave to take that girl in. Not many would have dared."

"You would have done the same," Mariah said softly. "You've too much heart to ignore someone in need."

Caroline smiled faintly. "Perhaps. But I do wonder how my brother will react when he hears of this. Oliver has never tolerated injustice, he'll be livid."

"Oliver is a good man," Mariah murmured, her voice faltering slightly as his name left her lips.

"That he is," Caroline agreed. A knock at the door interrupted them. Both women turned as Mrs. Parker stepped inside, her usual composure firmly in place.

Mariah smiled. "What is it, Mrs. Parker?"

"I came to ask whether you wish to take all your gowns with you, My Lady."

"Yes, please," Mariah replied. "It's best to be prepared."

Mrs. Parker, curtsied. "Very good," she said, before slipping quietly from the room. Caroline watched the door close.

"It's awfully kind of your housekeeper to see to the packing herself. I had expected we would do it together, with perhaps a few maids to assist."

"Mrs. Parker insisted," Mariah said with affection. "She's been with me since childhood, loyal to a fault. I shall miss her dreadfully." Tears shimmered in her eyes, and Caroline reached for her hand.

"I wish you didn't have to leave."

"Part of me doesn't want to," Mariah confessed softly. "I'll miss your company and friendship more than I can say. But let us not dwell on goodbyes. You'll soon be married, and happiness will find you again. We'll visit one another before long, I'm sure."

Another knock startled them both. A maid entered, curtsying, quickly.

"The Earl of Wyndham is here to see you, ma'am," she announced nervously. Caroline and Mariah exchanged alarmed glances.

"Thank you, Sophia," Mariah said, recovering her composure. "Inform Mr. Grayson and send the earl in."

As soon as the maid hurried out, Caroline rose from her chair.

"You cannot mean to see him alone."

"I won't be alone," Mariah replied, her voice calm but taut with fury. "You're here, and Mr. Grayson will be nearby. Let him come."

Before another word could be spoken, the door swung open and the Earl of Wyndham strode in. His dark eyes burned with anger, his expression thunderous. Though he bowed stiffly, his fury was barely contained.

"Miss Winter," he snapped, his voice echoing off the walls. "You are holding one of my servants against her will. I demand that you surrender her at once."

Mariah straightened. "I am protecting her from you, My Lord, not detaining her. And I would appreciate it if you lowered your voice in my house." Her composure only seemed to inflame him further.

"You would do well to remember your place," he retorted, his tone dripping with disdain. "Do not think the presence of Lady Caroline will restrain me. She and I are equals. You are not."

Mariah's eyes flashed.

"Lady Caroline Williams is engaged to the Marquess of Pedham," she said icily. "I daresay his title outranks yours, My Lord. And no amount of posturing will intimidate me."

The earl sneered. "Where is my maid?"

"She is not your maid," Mariah shot back. "She may have worked in your household, but she is not your property. You have wronged her shamefully. The very least you could do is ensure she and her child are cared for."

Lord Dalton laughed, a cruel, mirthless sound.

"Care for her? I owe her nothing. She has no proof that the bastard is mine. For all anyone knows, she's seduced half the footmen in Norfolk in her bid for comfort."

Mariah's fury boiled over.

"You are despicable," she cried. "You destroy a woman's honor, then slander her to save your own! You call yourself a gentleman, yet you behave like the lowest of cowards."

"Careful," he warned, stepping closer. "You've no evidence for such accusations."

"Evidence?" she repeated, trembling with righteous anger. "Her bruises are evidence enough. Her terror is evidence enough. A gentleman protects the weak. You are no such thing, My Lord."

"Mind your tongue," he hissed, his composure slipping. "I am the Earl of Wyndham—"

"And you are standing," Mariah interrupted coldly, "in the home of the Viscount of Hethersett. Whatever your rank, this is not your house. You have no right to trespass here, and I will thank you to leave at once."

Dalton's jaw clenched, his face darkening.

"Some viscount," he sneered. "Word in London says he's neck-deep in debt. A desperate man, hardly fit to—"

"That is none of your concern," Mariah cut in sharply. "Now get out of this house before I have you thrown out."

The earl's composure finally shattered. With a roar of rage, he crossed the room in two strides, seized Mariah by the throat, and slammed her against the wall.

Caroline screamed. "Let her go!"

Mariah clawed at his hand, struggling for air as his grip tightened. Her vision blurred, the world narrowing to Caroline's terrified cries and the thunder of her own heartbeat. And still, even as her breath faltered, Mariah's eyes burned with defiance.

"Mr. Grayson, footmen!" Caroline called out, then rushed forward, intending to intervene, but before she could reach them, the door burst open. The steward entered first, followed by the Earl of Norwich, the Marquess of Pedham, and several footmen.

"Step away from her at once, Dalton," Lord Williams commanded, his voice low and thunderous. "If you do not leave this instant, I will have you arrested."

Lord Dalton froze for a fraction of a second before sneering.

"You have no right to interfere, Williams."

Still, he released Mariah, stepping back as she crumpled slightly, gasping for air and clutching her throat.

"The two ladies are under our protection," Lord Camden said sharply, his voice laced with cold authority. "Mark my words, Dalton, you will pay dearly for this outrage."

The Earl of Wyndham's gaze darted around the room, but every face that met his was dark with anger. Even the servants standing near the door had their hands clenched, their expressions openly hostile. His jaw tightened. He knew he was outnumbered. With a growl of frustration, he turned on his heel and stormed out, the door slamming so hard behind him that the windows rattled.

Caroline was at Mariah's side in an instant. The young woman trembled violently, her breathing ragged. For a moment, it looked as though she might collapse altogether.

"Good heavens, Mariah," Caroline exclaimed, tears brimming in her eyes. "That could have ended so horribly, why did you provoke him so?" Her voice wavered with fear and frustration. Lord Camden stepped forward and placed a comforting arm around her shoulders.

"Easy, dearest," he murmured, his expression softening.

"Thank you, James," Caroline whispered, resting briefly against him. Meanwhile, Oliver stood before Mariah, his hands steadying her shoulders.

"Here, sit down," he said gently. He guided her to the settee, remaining crouched before her. "Why did you face him alone?"

Mariah met his gaze, her eyes glistening.

"I didn't intend to," she rasped. "He was announced, and propriety demanded that I receive him. I sent for Mr. Grayson, but—" She coughed, wincing, "everything happened so quickly." Her voice was hoarse, and she shivered despite the fire burning nearby. Before either man could respond, Mrs. Parker swept into the room. Seeing Mariah's reddened neck and pale face, she let out a horrified gasp. Without hesitation, she wrapped her arms around the young woman and held her tightly.

"Oh, my poor dear," the housekeeper cried. "That dreadful man ought to rot in the lowest pit of Hades for what he's done. I nearly burst through the door myself, but Mr. Grayson forbade any of us to interfere."

"Mr. Grayson did the right thing," Mariah said hoarsely. "The Earl of Wyndham is dangerous. He respects no one, least of all women."

"And yet," Oliver said quietly, "you stood up to him. Alone." He sank back into a nearby armchair, rubbing a hand over his face. "You are remarkable, Mariah, but you terrify me when you do such things." Turning to the housekeeper, he asked, "How is Dalton's maid?"

"She is recovering, My Lord," Mrs. Parker replied. "Still shaken, of course, but her injuries are not severe. The physician believes she will be well enough to travel to London when the time comes."

"Good," Oliver said simply, the relief evident in his tone. Mariah, still pale, reached out and touched his arm.

"Have you discovered where the Duke of Kent is currently staying?"

Oliver nodded. "As fortune would have it, he is in London, dining tomorrow evening with the Duke of Ashford and the Dowager Duchess. It seems fortune favors us."

Mariah and Caroline exchanged a look of surprise.

"What?" Oliver asked, lifting an eyebrow. Caroline folded her hands, suddenly sheepish.

"We have never met Lord Haywood, of course, but... his name often comes up in conversation among the ladies. And not always in flattering ways."

Mariah nodded. "I've heard the same whispers, even here in Norfolk. The young duke, they say, is cold, distant, unapproachable."

"Gossip," Lord Camden said with a dismissive wave. "Idle nonsense. I've met His Grace several times and found him nothing but honorable."

"Perhaps he is different among men," Caroline suggested delicately, though she lowered her gaze beneath her brother's stern look. Mariah tilted her head, curiosity overcoming her hesitation.

"But why would so many ladies speak poorly of him if there were no truth to it?"

Oliver gave a short laugh. "Because, my dear, the ladies of the ton thrive on scandal. One rumor whispered at a ball becomes gospel by morning. All it takes is a single slight, a missed dance, an ignored compliment, for wounded pride to turn vengeful."

Caroline arched a brow. "You think all women so delicate?"

"I think," Oliver replied with a teasing smile, "that some women take offense when a man refuses to flatter them. Perhaps one hoped for the duke's attention and did not receive it."

Lord Camden chuckled. "Indeed. The Duke of Kent inherited his title far too young, and the burden upon him is immense. Estates to manage, tenants to protect, sisters' futures to secure, he has little time for society, let alone courtship. When he attends a ball, it is to please his mother and sisters, not to pursue a wife. Naturally, the ladies resent it." He shook his head, still smiling faintly.

"Many seek the title and fortune, not the man himself. A duke uninterested in flirtation is a blow to their vanity."

Mariah regarded him thoughtfully.

"So, it is the same for you as well, Oliver? Women pursue you for your title rather than for who you are?"

Oliver hesitated, then smiled faintly.

"Yes, and no. I was thrust into my role after Father's death, much as the duke was. But a duke's burdens are far heavier, and his choices far fewer."

Mariah lowered her gaze, her heart twisting at the quiet weariness in his voice. In that moment, she understood more clearly than ever how power and privilege could be as much a prison as a gift. And yet, as she sat surrounded by her dearest friends, her throat still sore, her pulse still racing, she could not shake the growing certainty that her fate, and that of the mysterious Duke of Kent, were destined to collide.

5

The Truth Knocks

S aying goodbye to the servants, and to her dearest friend, the following morning proved one of the hardest things Mariah had ever done. The household had gathered upon the front steps to see her off, the chill of early dawn clinging to the air. Mrs. Parker stood nearest the door, dabbing her eyes with a lace handkerchief, her usual composure undone. Beside her, Mr. Grayson offered Mariah a dignified bow, formal as ever, yet the emotion in his eyes betrayed him far more than words could have.

Mariah paused before the carriage, her gaze lingering on the familiar faces that had shaped her life. These people had been her constant, her quiet guardians, her comfort, her home. The weight of leaving them pressed heavily upon her heart. She turned at last to Caroline and clasped her hands tightly, as though afraid to let go.

"Promise you'll write," Caroline whispered, her voice trembling despite her brave smile.

"I will," Mariah assured her softly. "Every chance I get."

Caroline's grip tightened. "This house will feel dreadfully empty without you."

Mariah swallowed past the ache in her throat. "And I shall miss you more than I can say. But when your wedding comes, I'll be there, no matter what. I would not miss that day for the world."

Caroline's eyes shimmered. She leaned forward and embraced her, holding on, for a heartbeat longer than propriety allowed. Then, with a final look at the house she had known all her life, Mariah gathered her skirts and stepped into the carriage. The door closed with a soft thud that sounded far too final, and as the driver took up the reins, she felt the first true weight of the journey settle upon her shoulders.

Ahead lay London, truth, and a future still uncertain, but behind her stood love, loyalty, and a past she would never forget.

As the carriage pulled away from Hethersett Manor, Mariah looked back through misted eyes at the only home she had ever known. Every stone, every tree seemed to whisper farewell, as though the estate itself mourned her departure.

The journey to London was long and wearisome. The weather grew colder with each passing mile, and though the roads were dry, the ruts and stones jolted the carriage unpleasantly. Still, they pressed on, arriving at the outskirts of the city by early evening, the sky already dimming beneath a gray blanket.

Their first stop was on a modest street where Martha's family lived. Oliver himself assisted the young woman from the carriage, ensuring she was safely delivered into her parents' arms. Martha's mother clung to her daughter, weeping openly with gratitude, while her father grasped Oliver's hand in a firm, heartfelt shake.

"God bless you, My Lord," the man said earnestly. "For protecting our girl and bringing her home to us."

Oliver inclined his head. "She is a brave young woman. Take good care of her."

Mariah embraced Martha and promised to send word once she found suitable employment for her. Still, she gently urged the girl to rest and take comfort in her family for a time before shouldering any new burdens.

Their next stop was Lady Isadora's townhouse. Oliver explained that news had reached him of her grandfather's grave condition, and he wished to be at her side during the old man's final hours.

Before parting, he turned to Mariah.

"The carriage and driver are yours for as long as you require them," he said. "And if things do not go well with the Duke of Kent," he added gently, "promise me you will come straight to my townhouse."

"I promise," she replied softly. He gave her a faint, reassuring smile before stepping down into the fading light, leaving her once more to the quiet weight of her thoughts, and to the uncertain future that awaited her in the city ahead.

By the time the carriage drew up before the grand iron gates of Lord Haywood's London residence, night had fully fallen. Gas lamps lined the street, casting a warm, golden glow over polished carriages and well-dressed passersby, their reflections shimmering against wet cobblestones.

Mariah's heart thudded painfully in her chest as she stepped down and looked up at the sprawling townhouse beyond the gates. Stately columns framed the entrance, and light glittered behind tall windows, hinting at warmth, power, and a life utterly foreign to her own.

The house possessed a commanding presence, quiet, dignified, and formidable, befitting one of the highest peers in England. She had imagined this moment countless times during the long journey south, rehearsing her words, steeling her resolve. Yet now that she stood before his home, uncertainty clawed at her composure. To arrive unannounced felt improper, almost reckless, but she had no alternative. A letter might be dismissed, ignored, or lost. Only her presence could force the truth into the open.

Perhaps, she reasoned, if she were received in the presence of servants, witnesses, her words would carry greater weight. Whatever his reaction, she would not be dismissed as easily. And whatever the outcome, she could not turn back now.

Drawing in a steadying breath, Mariah smoothed her gloved hands over her skirts and mounted the steps. The night air felt sharp against her cheeks as she raised her hand and grasped the heavy brass knocker. Her fingers trembled slightly, not from fear alone, but from the knowledge that with this single action, everything might change. She lifted the knocker and let it fall. The sound echoed through the house like a declaration of fate.

The door opened after a long pause. A tall butler stood there, his posture rigid, his expression guarded.

"Yes?" he asked curtly. Mariah forced her voice to remain steady.

"I am here to see His Grace, the Duke of Kent."

The man's eyes swept over her attire, her plain traveling cloak, her modest gown, the lack of any crest or calling card.

"Do you have an appointment?"

"No," she admitted.

"Is His Grace expecting you this evening?"

She shook her head again. "I'm afraid not."

Before the butler could respond, another man stepped forward, a broad-shouldered, self-important fellow whose manner suggested he relished authority far more than courtesy.

"Is there a problem, Gordon?"

"No, Mr. Swan," the butler replied. "This young lady wishes to see His Grace, Lord Kensington."

"Does she indeed?" The steward's gaze traveled over Mariah with unmistakable condescension. "And whom shall I say is calling?"

"My name is Mariah Kensington," she said clearly, lifting her chin. "I am the daughter of the Duke of Kent."

The two men exchanged a glance. A flicker of amusement passed between them, thinly veiled but unmistakable.

"Listen, miss," Mr. Swan began, his tone heavy with disdain, "we've heard that tale before. Every few months, some poor girl arrives claiming to be His Grace's long-lost daughter, hoping for charity or attention. It's quite tiresome."

Mariah bristled. "I am not lying. I have my birth record and other documents with me. If you will allow me a moment, I can show you—"

"There is no need," he cut in coldly. "We have no interest in fabricated papers. His Grace will not be disturbed by impostors tonight."

"I am not an impostor!" Her composure cracked, anger breaking through the restraint she had fought to maintain. "If you would only allow me to speak with him, even for a moment, he would know the truth."

"Enough," Mr. Swan snapped. "Leave at once, or I will have you removed. Gordon," he added sharply, "inform the staff that no one is to admit strangers or deliver messages to Lord Kensington while he remains in this house."

"Yes, sir."

The heavy door closed with a resounding thud. Mariah stood motionless on the steps, her pulse pounding, humiliation and fury warring within her. Slowly, she clenched her fists, her breath trembling.

"We shall see about that," she whispered fiercely. "If you think I'll give up so easily, you are sorely mistaken." She returned to the carriage and opened her smallest trunk, withdrawing some of the documents she had brought, the letters, the records, each one neatly folded and tucked into her reticule. With determination burning brighter than fear, she slipped back into the night and circled the grand townhouse, keeping close to the shadows.

It did not take long to notice a side door standing ajar, likely left open by servants seeking a breath of fresh air. Her heart raced as she crept closer, listening intently. Hearing nothing, she slipped inside and closed the door softly behind her.

The room beyond was dimly lit and vast, its walls lined with towering shelves. The rich, comforting scent of leather bindings and parchment filled the air. It was a library, and a magnificent one. For a fleeting moment, her fear gave way to awe. She ran her fingers along the spines of nearby books, breathing in the familiar perfume of old paper and candle wax. Then her elbow brushed a small table. The lamp teetered, then crashed to the floor with a sharp, shattering clang. Mariah gasped and darted behind a bookshelf, pressing herself flat against the wood as panic surged through her veins. Footsteps thundered down the corridor. The door burst open, flooding the room with light.

"Is someone in here?" came a deep voice, Gordon, the butler. Another set of footsteps followed.

"What is it, Gordon?" Mr. Swan demanded sharply.

"I heard something shatter," the butler replied, scanning the room. His gaze landed on the broken lamp. "There it is."

Swan stepped inside, irritation etched across his face. Just then, a gust of cold air swept through the room, setting the curtains billowing dramatically.

"There's your culprit, I'd say," he muttered, striding toward the window to shut it. Mariah pressed her hand over her mouth, scarcely daring to breathe, her pulse hammering so loudly she feared it might betray her.

Mariah seized the brief opportunity while the two men's backs were turned. Moving silently along the row of shelves, she reached the open door and slipped through it, her pulse hammering in her ears. With trembling fingers, she closed the door behind her and turned the key in the lock, trapping them both inside.

Almost at once, a roar of outrage echoed from within the library.

"What is this?" the steward bellowed, rattling the handle. "Open this door at once! What the devil is going on here?"

Mariah pressed her lips together to keep from laughing. The sound of his indignant fury was almost worth the risk she had taken. She hurried down the corridor, her soft slippers barely whispering against the polished floorboards. But her triumph was short-lived. She had gone only a few paces, when footsteps approached from the opposite direction. Panic flared. She glanced around for an escape and darted toward a nearby door, intending to slip through unnoticed.

A strong hand caught her by the arm.

"Let go of me!" she gasped, twisting in protest. Her captor said nothing. Instead, he turned her effortlessly and hoisted her over his shoulder as though she weighed nothing at all. She let out a startled cry, her fists pounding uselessly against his back. Within moments, he carried her into a richly appointed study and deposited her unceremoniously into a deep armchair.

Mariah shot upright, ready to bolt, but he pressed her gently, yet firmly, back into the seat with one hand.

"Stay," he said, his tone brooking no argument. She froze, less from fear than astonishment. The man standing before her was tall and powerfully built, with a presence that filled the room. Warm brown eyes, keen and intelligent, studied her closely beneath dark brows. Firelight caught in his dark hair, illuminating a strong jaw and a mouth that was stern yet undeniably handsome. Her heart fluttered traitorously.

My word... Surely this could not be her father, he was far too young. Which meant only one thing. This was the Duke of Ashford's heir. Lord Haywood himself. He crossed his arms and leaned casually against the edge of his desk.

"Who are you," he demanded, "and what, precisely, are you doing in my house?"

Mariah opened her mouth to answer, but the door burst open, and the steward stormed in, his face red with fury.

"You!" he spat, glaring at her. "You insolent little—" He took a step forward, but the younger man raised a hand, stopping him short.

"Let her speak, Amistad," the duke said evenly.

"She was at the front door earlier, Your Grace," Amistad said tightly. "She claimed to be the Duke of Kent's daughter. When we refused her entry, she apparently decided to sneak into the house instead."

"I tried to explain that I have proof," Mariah shot back, glaring at the steward. "But you wouldn't even let me finish a sentence. I've traveled all the way from Norwich to meet my father. I was not about to turn back simply because you didn't believe me."

Lord Haywood studied her intently, his brow furrowing.

"If you are truly his daughter," he said, "why come forward only now?"

"Because I only learned the truth days ago," Mariah replied steadily. "The couple who raised me kept my identity hidden from everyone, including me. I discovered who I am through a letter left behind after my mother's death."

"And you expect us to believe such a story?" Amistad demanded, skepticism dripping from every word. Mariah drew herself up.

"It does not matter whether *you* believe me," she said coolly. "The Duke of Kent is the only one who needs to."

A faint smile touched the corner of Lord Haywood's mouth, though his eyes remained guarded.

"You must understand," he said slowly, "His Grace has suffered greatly because of false claims. Many women have come forward pretending to be his lost daughter. Each time, his hopes were raised, only to be shattered. He and my late father were the closest of friends. I will not see him wounded again." Her voice softened.

"I do not wish to hurt him, only to know him. My entire life has been turned upside down, and he is the only one who can help me make sense of it. Tell me, Your Grace, if you discovered the family who raised you was not your own, would you not seek the truth?"

Something flickered in his expression, sympathy, perhaps, or reluctant admiration. She reached into her reticule and withdrew a small bundle of papers.

"Here," she said quietly, extending the first paper with steady hands. "This is the birth record from the day I was born." She hesitated only a moment before unfolding the second document. "And this is the false one, the record created by the woman who took me."

Lord Haywood accepted the papers and examined them with care, his expression tightening as he read. The longer he studied the inked lines, the deeper the crease in his brow became. Without a word, he passed the documents to Amistad, who scowled openly but took them, nonetheless.

"They appear genuine," the duke murmured at last, his voice thoughtful rather than dismissive.

Relief fluttered through Mariah's chest, though she did not allow herself to show it.

"You could also tell him that my nursemaid, Clarice, was the one who took me and raised me as her own," she added quietly. "Perhaps he still remembers her name. And I have more, her diary, correspondence, and additional documents, in one of my trunks. If you will permit it, I can have them brought inside."

"We do not trouble the household staff on behalf of strangers," Amistad interrupted sharply. "If you wish to retrieve your evidence, you may do so yourself."

The words struck harder than she expected. Mariah drew a careful breath, swallowing as pride wrestled with hurt. Even if she had been nothing more than a servant, she deserved courtesy. *Was this the vaunted ton of London,* she wondered bitterly, *a world so blinded by rank that it forgot the meaning of decency altogether?* She straightened, refusing to let the slight diminish her.

"Very well," she said quietly, her voice composed despite the heat behind her eyes. "If I retrieve the documents myself, will you allow me back into the house?" Her gaze met the duke's, clear, resolute, and unflinching. Lord Haywood studied her for a heartbeat longer, as though weighing more than her request. Then he nodded.

"Yes."

"Then I shall return shortly," Mariah said simply. She turned to leave, but his hand closed around her arm again, firm, not rough. Startled by the warmth of his touch, she stopped.

"Where are you going?" he asked, a hint of amusement in his voice.

"To the carriage," she replied coolly. "I need my trunk."

He exchanged an incredulous glance with his steward.

"You intend to carry it in yourself?"

Her eyes flashed. "You think I can't?" she snapped. "I assure you, Your Grace, I am quite capable of lifting a trunk without assistance."

She removed his hand with deliberate grace, her chin lifted proudly. For a heartbeat, silence reigned, then both men burst out laughing. Mariah spun back toward them, mortified.

"You think this amusing? That *I* am?"

Lord Haywood raised a hand, still smiling.

"Not at all. I think you're extraordinary. Most women would have fainted by now. You, however, threaten to outwit half my household."

Amistad grinned. "To be fair, young lady, I would never have allowed you to carry it alone. We may have seemed ungentlemanly, but I was merely testing your mettle."

"Testing me?" she echoed incredulously.

He bowed slightly. "I would help any lady in distress, even one trespassing through the back door."

Mariah wasn't certain whether to be flattered or furious.

"How very noble of you," she muttered dryly.

Lord Haywood chuckled. "Enough, Amistad. Send word for the footmen to bring the young lady's trunks inside. I will take her to the duke myself."

Amistad's brows rose. "Your Grace, are you certain?"

"Quite." Lord Haywood turned back to Mariah and extended his arm. "Come, Miss Kensington. Let us see whether your documents convince His Grace as thoroughly as your determination has convinced me."

Mariah hesitated, searching his eyes for mockery, but found only warmth, and something very much like respect.

"And if the proof I have is not enough?" she asked softly. His smile was genuine, disarming, and it made her heart stumble.

"Then I shall not cast you back into the cold," he said. "Whatever the truth may be, I believe you deserve to be heard."

Mariah drew a steadying breath and placed her hand upon his arm. As he led her from the room, she could not decide which unsettled her more, the fear of meeting the man who might be her father... or the dangerous charm of the man walking beside her.

"Garrett, what took you so long?" the Dowager Duchess of Kent asked, arching an elegant brow at her son. "You said you only meant to see what caused the noise."

Garrett offered her a faintly mischievous smile, though his eyes were thoughtful.

"And I did, Mother. Forgive me for taking longer than expected, but I have brought someone who wishes to see His Grace."

He turned toward the doorway. Lord Kensington, who had been standing near the fire in quiet conversation, lifted his head in mild curiosity. The change in his expression was immediate, and profound, the moment Mariah stepped into the room. The color drained from his face as though struck by an unseen hand.

The steward followed her in but halted just inside the threshold, suddenly unsure of his place.

The Duke of Kent's breath caught audibly. He took an unsteady step forward. His gaze fixed upon Mariah as though he were seeing a ghost made flesh. Behind him, an older woman, white-haired, dignified, and regal despite the tremor in her limbs, staggered closer, one hand flying to her throat.

"Cecelia..." the duke whispered, his voice breaking on the name. The woman beside him echoed it, scarcely louder than a breath.

"Cecelia?"

Mariah froze mid-step, the sound of her own name, or something close enough to it, echoing through her mind like a bell struck too hard. A stunned silence swept across the drawing room, thick and heavy, pressing in from all sides. Garrett sensed the moment at once. With a subtle nod, he dismissed the steward. The man bowed quickly and slipped from the room, closing the door softly behind him.

The fire crackled. The lamps burned low. And in that charged stillness, Mariah stood face-to-face with the past, one heartbeat away from learning whether the truth she carried would shatter a family... or restore it.

6

A Gown Fit for a Princess

Lord Kensington moved forward slowly, disbelief and wonder warring across his face. His eyes glistened, and when he finally found his voice, it was hoarse with emotion.

"Are you...?" He hesitated, searching her face as though afraid the vision before him might vanish. "Are you my daughter, Mariah?"

Mariah's throat tightened. She managed a small nod. A strangled sound escaped him, half sob, half laugh and in the next instant, he closed the distance between them, gathering her into his arms.

"My dearest girl," he whispered brokenly. "You look just like your mother."

The embrace undid her completely. Lord Winter had often been affectionate, but never like this. The warmth, the strength, the *rightness* of it flooded through her. For the first time in her life, she felt as though she belonged, utterly and without condition. Tears spilled down her cheeks as she clung to him, her heart swelling with joy and grief all at once. How could a man she had never met make her feel so safe, so cherished, so profoundly *home*?

Neither spoke for several long moments. When at last they drew apart, the duke lifted her chin gently, his eyes, like her own, filled with tenderness.

"There you are," he murmured, studying her face as though committing every detail to memory. "My beautiful daughter."

Mariah blushed, overwhelmed by the intensity of his gaze, yet comforted by the love that radiated from him, steady, certain, and real.

Forcing himself to look away before emotion overtook him once more, James drew a steadying breath and turned toward his mother.

"Mother," he said softly, his voice still thick with feeling, "I would like you to meet your granddaughter."

The Dowager Duchess's composure faltered at once. Tears glistened in her eyes as she approached Mariah, taking her hands as though afraid, she might disappear. Then she drew her into a tight embrace, holding her close.

"My dear child," she whispered, her voice trembling. "I never believed I would live to see this day, to see James reunited with his daughter." She pulled back only far enough to study Mariah's face, her gaze lingering with awe and tenderness.

"And he is right," she said, a fragile smile breaking through her tears. "You look so very much like Cecelia that, for one dizzy moment, I thought it was your mother standing before me. The likeness is uncanny." Her expression softened further as she sighed. "If only your grandfather could have witnessed this... he would have been overcome with joy."

Mariah's heart swelled anew, so much love offered freely by people who had been strangers only moments before yet were her family by blood and by bond. She murmured her gratitude, though the words felt wholly inadequate to express the depth of what she felt.

The Duke of Ashford introduced Mariah to his mother and his two younger sisters. Each of the ladies curtsied warmly, their expressions filled with wonder and heartfelt kindness.

"We have prayed for you," the elder of the two sisters said softly. "Even when hope felt foolish, we never stopped believing you might still be alive."

"Yes," the younger added with a tremulous smile. "You are already family to us. Nothing could ever change that."

Mariah felt her throat tighten once more. The warmth of their acceptance, the ease with which she was drawn into their circle, left her breathless. She managed to say a quiet word of thanks, her voice unsteady with emotion.

Sensing that Mariah was both exhausted and overwhelmed, the Duke of Kent wisely decided to postpone any discussion of her past until later. The questions would come, there were so many of them, but not yet.

"Come," he said gently, offering her his arm. "You must be famished. There will be time enough for answers after dinner." His voice was warm, reassuring, and unmistakably paternal. Mariah hesitated, only a heartbeat before placing her hand upon his sleeve. He smiled down at her, a smile filled with quiet pride and something very like awe, and though her nerves fluttered at the thought of what lay ahead, she returned the smile.

For the first time since discovering the truth of her birth, she allowed herself to feel something close to peace. Whatever questions awaited her, she would face them not alone but surrounded by family and friends and guided by the steady presence of the man who was, at last, truly her father.

Dinner passed in a gentle blur of candlelight, conversation, and warmth. The long mahogany table gleamed beneath crystal chandeliers, their light dancing across polished silver as footmen moved with quiet grace about the room.

Mariah found herself seated beside her father, with the dowager duchess across from them and Lord Haywood presiding at the head of the table. Every so often, she glanced at her father, scarcely able to believe that this man, so commanding, so kind, was truly hers.

He was tall and broad-shouldered, undeniably handsome, his dark brown hair threaded with dignified silver. His eyes, gentle yet penetrating, seemed to take in everything at once. There was strength in him, yes, but also patience, restraint, and a quiet attentiveness that made her feel seen without scrutiny.

Her grandmother, elegant despite her years, conversed easily with her, drawing her into the rhythm of the table and making her feel welcome with every word. Though her hair was white as snow, she retained the regal bearing of a woman who had once ruled drawing rooms, and, Mariah suspected, still could when she chose. For Mariah, the evening unfolded like a dream she feared might vanish at any moment, a daze of wonder, warmth, and belonging unlike anything she had ever known.

After dinner, the men declined their usual port and, without ceremony, joined the ladies in the drawing room. The shift felt deliberate, as though no one wished to break the fragile intimacy of the evening by retreating behind tradition. Once everyone had settled, chairs drawn closer, the fire crackling softly, James turned to his daughter with quiet intensity.

"Tell me everything," he said gently. "Your life... and how you came to discover the truth."

Mariah drew a steadying breath and began. She spoke of her childhood with the Winters, of a home filled with structure and affection, of guidance and care that had shaped her into the woman she was. She did not spare them kindness, even now. She spoke honestly of her shock upon discovering the letter, the diary, the confession that had shattered one identity and revealed another. Her voice wavered only once, when she described the moment she realized her name, her heritage, her very place in the world had never truly been her own.

Throughout her account, the Duke of Kent did not interrupt. His expression shifted with each revelation, sorrow softening into gratitude, disbelief giving way to awe. Halfway through her story, he reached for her hand, his grip firm and reassuring, as though grounding them both. He did not release it until she finished. When at last her words fell into silence, he spoke quietly.

"You have endured some serious betrayal," he said. "And yet you speak of it with such grace, without bitterness." His voice thickened. "I cannot tell you how proud I am of you, my dear girl."

Tears shimmered once more in Mariah's eyes. She squeezed his hand, overwhelmed by the warmth of his words, by the certainty of his acceptance. And yet, even as she basked in the comfort of her father's presence, she found her gaze drifting, repeatedly, toward the Duke of Ashford. He sat slightly apart from the others, his posture relaxed yet attentive, his head inclined as he listened. Firelight danced across his features, casting soft shadows along the strong line of his jaw, the curve of his mouth, the thoughtful depth of his eyes.

Mariah tried to resist the pull of her attention but failed. The resemblance between him and her father was unmistakable. Both men possessed that same effortless authority, that quiet strength that did not demand attention yet commanded it all the same. She wondered, fleetingly, whether her mother had once looked at her father with the same mixture of admiration and uncertainty now stirring within her own heart.

As the evening wore on, Mariah found herself suspended between two powerful truths: the joy of discovering her family at last, and the unsettling realization that the man who had led her to them stirred emotions she could scarcely name, emotions she was not yet ready to examine. For now, she told herself, it was enough simply to belong. But even as she leaned back in her chair, wrapped in warmth and newfound love, she sensed that this was only the beginning, that her life, newly claimed, was already bending toward a future far more complicated, and far more compelling, than she had ever imagined.

The news of the return of Lord Kensington's daughter, and her long-awaited reunion with her father spread through London society and all of England like wildfire. Within hours, the gossip sheets buzzed with speculation, and the drawing rooms of Mayfair hummed with eager chatter. By the following morning, invitations and calling cards had begun to pour in from nearly every corner of the ton. Curious acquaintances, hopeful debutantes, and even the occasional dowager desperate for fresh intrigue all sought an introduction to Lady Mariah Kensington, the duke's miraculously restored daughter.

But those hoping to catch a glimpse of her at the Kent townhouse were destined for disappointment. Determined to shield her granddaughter from the frenzy, the Dowager Duchess had spirited Mariah away for the day, to Watford, where she might shop for new gowns and acclimate herself to her new station in relative peace. They were joined by the Dowager Duchess of Ashford and her two daughters, Lady Agnes and Lady Nora.

The day passed in a whirl of activity and delight. Mariah, who had never known such luxury, found herself surrounded by silks and satins, ribbons and lace in every imaginable hue. The duchesses and shopkeepers fussed over her measurements, debating colors that would best flatter her complexion, soft lavender, blush rose, and deep blue to bring out her eyes.

At first, Mariah felt overwhelmed by the attention, uncertain how to carry herself amid so much finery and expectation. But the warmth and genuine affection of the women soon put her at ease. The Dowager Duchess of Ashford, graceful and maternal, treated her as though she had always belonged among them, while Lord Haywood's sisters offered gentle guidance in the subtle art of choosing fabrics and trimmings worthy of a duke's daughter. Yet it was with Lady Nora, the youngest of the Haywood sisters, that Mariah felt the strongest connection.

Nora's spirit was bright and unpretentious, her laughter infectious. The two young women quickly discovered they shared much in common, an affection for the countryside, a preference for quiet reading overcrowded balls, and an irreverent sense of humor when it came to London's endless parade of social pretensions. Before the afternoon was over, they were conversing like old friends, trying on bonnets and gloves, giggling over daring styles they both admired but dared not purchase.

When the group paused for tea at a charming little tearoom, Mariah found herself seated between the two duchesses, listening as they reminisced about her mother. Their recollections were tender and vivid, Cecelia's laughter, her kindness, the way she had adored her husband and infant daughter. Mariah's heart swelled with gratitude. Though she had been deprived of her mother's presence, she realized she had inherited a family rich in love and memory, and in their company, she no longer felt like an outsider.

By late afternoon, the carriage was brimming with hatboxes, folded fabrics, and carefully wrapped parcels. As they made their way back toward London, Mariah gazed out at the passing countryside, her heart light. For the first time in years, she felt that her life, once shattered by loss and deceit, was beginning, at last, to find its shape again.

That evening, the Kensington townhouse was filled with light and laughter. Two of the duke's brothers and their families joined them for dinner, along with a few close friends eager to meet the long-lost daughter whose return had stirred both hearts, and gossip, throughout London. Mariah soon discovered that she had several cousins near her own age, and to her delight, they took to one another at once. The two eldest daughters of Lord Kensington's second-eldest brother, Aurelia and Elsie, seemed especially determined to make her feel welcome.

"It is so good to finally meet you, Mariah," Aurelia said warmly, her smile radiant. "I don't believe I've ever seen Uncle James so happy."

"That's true," Elsie agreed with equal enthusiasm. "Father said earlier that Uncle hasn't looked this joyful since before Aunt Cecelia passed."

Mariah's expression softened. "I wish I had known my mother," she murmured wistfully. Elsie reached across the table and touched her arm gently. "We have only ever heard the kindest things about the late Duchess of Kent. She was said to be one of the sweetest and most gracious ladies in all London. And Uncle James is right you look just like her."

Mariah smiled faintly. "Perhaps I've inherited her features," she said, "but I fear not her temperament. The gentleman who raised me, Lord Winter, used to call me headstrong and stubborn more often than not." She gave a rueful chuckle. "Perhaps sweetness skips a generation."

Both cousins laughed, their eyes bright.

"Don't be so hard on yourself," Aurelia said kindly. "We're all our own severest critics."

Their conversation was interrupted when new guests entered the drawing room. The Duke of Kent rose at once to greet them, his voice carrying warmly across the chamber. Curious, Mariah followed the exchange with interest.

"Are you wondering who they are?" Elsie asked, noting her cousin's attentive gaze. Before Mariah could reply, she continued eagerly, "The older lady is Lady Constance Haywood, Dowager

Duchess of Ashford. With her are her daughters, Lady Agnes and Lady Nora. And the young gentleman just behind them is—"

"Lord Garrett Haywood, the Duke of Ashford," Mariah finished softly, a knowing smile curving her lips.

Elsie blinked in surprise. "You've met him already?"

"I have," Mariah replied quietly. "He and his family dined with my father when I first arrived."

Elsie grinned. "Then you've met one of London's most sought-after bachelors. Don't you think him handsome?"

Mariah's cheeks warmed. "Yes... he is very handsome," she admitted before she could stop herself. Elsie's grin widened.

"Very handsome, and much admired."

Before Mariah could recover, her father approached, the Haywoods following close behind. She rose at once and dipped into a graceful curtsy.

"It is a pleasure to see you again, Lady Haywood," she said politely. The dowager duchess smiled fondly.

"Considering we spent the entire day shopping together, my dear, such formality is quite unnecessary."

Lord Haywood stepped forward then, bowing lightly.

"Lady Mariah."

She returned the gesture, though her composure wavered when she met his gaze. His expression, known only to himself, yet so intent, sent an unwelcome, and unmistakable, warmth to her cheeks.

"I understand you enjoyed your outing with my mother and sisters," he said, his tone courteous, touched with amusement.

"I did indeed," Mariah replied. "They made me feel most welcome, and I thank you for allowing them to spend the day with me."

"I would hardly have denied them the pleasure," he said easily, his smile quickening her pulse. Agnes and Nora soon drew Mariah into conversation once introductions were complete.

"What a blessing that we are already acquainted," Lady Nora said brightly. "Had we met for the first time at the ball, there would have been no chance for proper conversation, half of London will be vying for your attention."

"The ball?" Mariah repeated, blinking. The sisters exchanged amused looks.

"You mean your father hasn't told you?" Agnes asked.

"We've scarcely had time to speak today," Mariah replied with a small laugh.

"It is the final grand ball before Christmastide," Agnes explained. "Your father hosts it every year. Many return to town for it before retreating to their country estates."

Aurelia leaned closer, her voice gentle.

"And this year, it is held in your honor."

"In my honor?" Mariah echoed, startled. "But why?"

"Because it was around this time that you were taken from him," Aurelia said softly. "Each year he held the ball to honor your memory, and to keep hope alive. It was also a promise he made to the late Duke of Ashford, to watch over his daughters." She nodded fondly toward Agnes and Nora.

"For the past two years," Elsie added, "your father has purchased a gown for his missing daughter. Each time, it was gifted to a deserving young lady of modest means, allowing her to attend the ball as a special guest."

Mariah's throat tightened. "How very kind of him." Her gaze drifted across the room to where her father stood among the gentlemen, speaking animatedly. Her heart swelled. "He must be a remarkable man."

"The ball is the day after tomorrow," Elsie added.

"So soon?" Mariah gasped. "Is it even possible to have a gown made in time?"

"Didn't you go shopping today?" Aurelia asked.

"We did," Lady Agnes said, "but nothing suitable for a formal presentation to society."

Before Mariah could fret, her grandmother joined them, smiling knowingly.

"There is no cause for concern, my dear. Your father ordered a gown weeks ago. One he insisted would be fit for a princess. The young lady who was meant to receive it this year shall instead wear one of the gowns I purchased today."

Mariah blinked. "Could I not wear that one instead?"

"Oh no," the dowager duchess said gently but firmly. "You are to be presented properly."

Mariah laughed softly. "So, why does the ton wish to meet me? Is it simply because I am my father's daughter?"

Lady Nora grinned. "That is certainly part of it, but you will also be the subject of every gossiping tongue in London."

"And," Mariah added dryly, "a fine piece of meat for the suitor population."

The young women burst into laughter. As their mirth echoed through the room, Mariah noticed Lord Haywood watching from nearby. A faint, amused smirk curved his lips, deepening when their eyes met. He inclined his head in a teasing bow, sending a fresh rush of color to her cheeks.

"Oh, Lady Mariah," Lady Nora said, looping her arm through hers. "You are utterly delightful. London will adore you."

Startled but pleased, Mariah allowed herself to be drawn closer, her earlier nerves dissolving into laughter. Perhaps, she thought, with a flutter of hope, London society... and its most intriguing duke... might not be quite as dreadful as she had feared.

The evening of the ball arrived with all the pomp and anticipation London society could muster. From the moment Mariah awoke that morning, her nerves fluttered relentlessly, a heady mixture of excitement, dread, and sheer disbelief. For hours, the household had been a whirlwind of activity. Servants hurried through the corridors, florists arrived bearing arrangements of white roses and lilies, and the grand chandeliers were polished until they gleamed like captured starlight.

It was the first Kensington Ball in years to be held with joy rather than grief, and all of London knew the reason why. Lady Mariah Kensington, the duke's long-lost daughter, was to make her official debut. That morning, she had begged her father to allow her to engage Martha as her chambermaid, and he had agreed without hesitation. The young maid entered her service that very afternoon, shy, earnest, and determined to please.

Together with two of the household's experienced chambermaids, Martha spent hours arranging Mariah's hair, fastening her jewels, and ensuring that every fold of her gown lay in perfect order. When at last Mariah looked into the mirror, she scarcely recognized the young woman reflected there. Her golden hair had been swept into a soft, elegant twist, with delicate curls framing her face. Loose tendrils caught the candlelight like spun silk. Her gown, pale blue satin embroidered with silver thread, fit her as though it had been fashioned solely for her. The neckline was modest yet flattering, and the skirts shimmered faintly with every breath she took.

"You look divine, My Lady," Martha whispered, stepping back to admire her work. Mariah smiled softly.

"Thank you, Martha. I'm so glad you're here with me tonight."

Her thoughts drifted briefly to her cousins, Aurelia and Elsie, who were unable to attend due to a wedding on their mother's side. The disappointment lingered like a small ache, but she took comfort in knowing that Nora and Agnes would soon arrive. Their easy laughter and steady companionship would be her anchor amid a sea of strangers and curious eyes.

As the hour drew near, Mariah stood by the window, gazing down at the glittering procession of carriages arriving below. Music, laughter, and the clatter of hooves rose from the courtyard as London's elite poured in, ladies shimmering in silk and lace, gentlemen resplendent in dark coats and polished boots. Her heart thudded wildly as she turned away from the window. Any moment now, her father would summon her. And then, at last, the knock came.

7

Whispers in the Garden

When Mariah entered the ballroom, a hush rippled through the crowd. Conversation stilled, fans paused mid-flutter, and every gaze turned toward her as she crossed the marble floor to stand beside her father. The Duke of Kent looked down at her with unmistakable pride as he took her hand and guided her toward the dais. His voice carried clearly above the soft swell of music and murmured anticipation.

"May I present to you, my friends and peers, my daughter, Lady Mariah Kensington."

Polite applause filled the room, refined and measured, yet beneath the civility Mariah could feel the full weight of their scrutiny, the curiosity, the comparisons, the whispered speculation already taking shape behind gloved hands. She held her smile steadily, though her fingers trembled faintly at her sides.

The orchestra struck the opening notes of a waltz, and her father drew her smoothly into his arms, opening the ball himself. The familiar rhythm steadied her, and for a moment she felt safe, anchored by his strength. The Duke of Kent held her with quiet confidence, smiling proudly at his daughter as they moved across the floor. When the music came to an end and before she could take more than a single breath, a young gentleman stepped forward to claim the next set. Mariah recognized him only vaguely, someone's heir, perhaps a viscount's son. He bowed deeply, his smile brimming with self-assurance.

"Lady Mariah, may I have the honor?"

She inclined her head with practiced grace.

"Of course."

They joined the other couples, upon the floor. Mariah moved effortlessly, her steps precise, years of instruction from a determined governess serving her well, but her thoughts drifted far from the cadence of the music. The room felt too bright, too crowded, too expectant. Every glance seemed to weigh her worth, every smile to measure her fortune. Each man who approached wished to claim her hand, not her heart. And after the quiet ache left by Oliver's loss, she found the thought of placing her trust in another utterly exhausting.

When the third set concluded, Mariah curtsied to her partner and murmured her thanks. At the first moment propriety allowed, she slipped away, weaving through the press of guests and escaping unnoticed through the great double doors that opened onto the gardens. Cool night air greeted her like a blessing. She breathed deeply as she stepped into the shadowed paths beyond the glow of lanterns, grateful for the quiet, and for the brief freedom from a world that suddenly expected far more of her than she felt ready to give.

The sky was clear and vast, the stars glittering like scattered diamonds over the lantern-lit lawns. Behind her, laughter and music drifted through the open doors in a warm, distant hum, but out here, the world seemed to pause. The press of expectation loosened its grip, and for the first time since entering the ballroom, she could think.

She descended the marble steps and followed the path that curved toward the rose gardens, her slippers whispering softly against the gravel. The scent of late blooms lingered in the air, mingled with the crisp bite of approaching winter. It was a fragrance she found grounding, real, unpretentious, untouched by chandeliers and whispered judgments. Then she froze. From beyond the corner of the house came the unmistakable sound of carriage wheels and animated voices. Guests were still arriving.

Startled, Mariah glanced around and quickly slipped behind a large ornamental shrub near the entrance, tucking herself into its shadow. The last thing she desired was to be discovered wandering alone like a restless child, already overwhelmed by her own debut. From her hiding place, she watched as a familiar carriage rolled to a stop.

Relief, and something like happiness, flooded her chest as Lady Haywood stepped down, followed by Nora and Agnes, both radiant in gowns of cream and lavender that glowed softly beneath the lanterns. Mariah nearly called out to them before remembering herself. Just then, a ripple of high, breathless laughter swept around the corner. She sank lower behind the shrub, suppressing a groan.

Goodness gracious, she thought. *The very last thing I need is to be caught eavesdropping like some mischievous debutante.*

The young ladies halted only a few paces away, their bright laughter softening into eager whispers. Mariah barely dared to breathe. And then the words reached her. Her heart sank as she realized, with sudden, chilling clarity, that they were speaking of her.

"Oh, look who has just arrived," one of the young ladies drawled, her voice dripping with spiteful amusement. "Lady Nora and Lady Agnes Haywood, and, of course, their impossibly proud mother."

Another gave a scoffing laugh.

"Those two will never find husbands. Everyone knows they've rejected half the eligible bachelors in London. Then they conveniently vanished after their father died. So ungrateful. And so peculiar."

A third voice, clear, steady, and unafraid, cut through the shrill commentary like a blade.

"Gossips such as you may repeat those tales," the young woman said coolly, "but that does not make them true. And for your information, they were not hiding. They were in mourning."

Mariah tilted her head, curiosity stirring. She rose slightly onto her toes, peering through the branches to glimpse the speaker.

"Mourning for two years?" the first girl scoffed again, disbelief heavy in her tone.

"Why not?" came the firm reply. "Perhaps they loved their father deeply and chose to honor him longer than the fashionable six months you find so convenient."

"Oh, Lady Elnora," sneered another, her tone sharp with derision. "If you admire them so greatly, why not go and join them?"

"I don't mind if I do," the young woman answered calmly. Mariah smiled despite herself as the speaker, a petite lady with fiery red hair braided in a coronet about her head, turned on her heel and walked away. Her posture was proud, her step purposeful, and the breeze caught a few loose curls, sending them dancing about her resolute face as she strode toward the house without a backward glance.

That one, Mariah thought with quiet admiration, *is worth knowing.* The remaining ladies clustered together again, their voices lowered but still sharp with irritation.

"And here comes His Grace," one murmured, hastily smoothing her skirts. "The Duke of Ashford himself. I cannot fathom why he even troubles himself to attend such gatherings. He never dances, never flirts, never even smiles. He spends half his life shut away at Ashford while his poor mother and sisters are left to endure London alone. No woman will ever be good enough for him."

Mariah followed their gaze just in time to see Lord Haywood step down from his carriage. Even at a distance, his presence was unmistakable. Tall and broad-shouldered, he carried himself with an effortless authority that drew the eye without any conscious effort. His expression was composed, unreadable, yet there was an intensity to him, a quiet gravity that set him apart from the other gentlemen arriving in a flurry of laughter and bravado.

She understood, suddenly, what the ladies meant by his reserve. During dinner at her father's house, he had spoken little, his words measured and precise, his gaze thoughtful and often inscrutable. And yet, for all their whispers and judgments, none of these young women knew him any better than she did.

Still, Mariah thought with a faint inward smile, it was curious that Caroline, or any of the ladies of Norwich, had never mentioned just how extraordinarily handsome the Duke of Ashford was. From her hiding place among the shrubs, she watched him ascend the steps, unaware that he was already the subject of speculation, and perhaps something far more dangerous than gossip, within her own quietly racing heart.

"Perhaps Lady Mariah will be the one," another of the girls mused, a speculative gleam lighting her eyes. "The late Duke of Ashford and the Duke of Kent were friends, were they not? I imagine the late duke would have approved of such a match. How poetic, to unite the two families."

The first young lady gave a derisive laugh, her tone dripping with contempt.

"As if Lord Kensington's daughter is anything remarkable. Pretty, yes, but from what I hear, she's as proud as the Haywoods. Perhaps she'll attach herself to them out of arrogance and become friends with them, but I doubt she'll ever rise above their company."

That was enough. Mariah stepped out from behind the hedge, her posture straight and unyielding, her eyes blazing with quiet fury. The movement startled the group. They whirled around as one, faces blanching as recognition dawned.

"I am already friends with Lady Nora and Lady Agnes," Mariah announced, her voice clear, steady, and ringing with authority. A sharp hush fell over them.

"Tell me," she continued, each word precise as cut crystal, "do you truly have nothing better to occupy your time than speaking ill of people you have never bothered to know? Does it give you comfort to wound others from behind their backs?" Her gaze swept over them coolly. "Or is it simply that you lack the courage to speak such things aloud, face to face?"

No one answered. A stunned silence followed. Fans fluttered nervously, gloved hands tightened, and panicked glances darted from one face to another, but not a single young lady dared to reply.

Unbeknownst to Mariah, her voice had carried farther than she realized. Across the drive, Lord Haywood had paused mid-step, one polished boot hovering just above the gravel. Conversation around him faded as his attention sharpened, drawn unerringly toward the source of the disturbance. His gaze found her at once, standing tall beneath the lantern light, chin lifted, eyes blazing with quiet authority, as one of his footmen halted beside him in startled confusion. For a moment, he did not move.

He watched as the cluster of young ladies stood frozen before her, their earlier bravado utterly extinguished. He noted Mariah's posture, unflinching, composed, unmistakably resolute. There was no shrillness in her rebuke, no desperation to be heard. Only truth, delivered with calm precision. A faint, almost imperceptible change crossed his expression. Approval. Perhaps even admiration.

At last, as if satisfied by what he had witnessed, Lord Haywood inclined his head ever so slightly, an acknowledgment meant for no one, and resumed his stride toward the house, his pace unhurried, his bearing thoughtful. Behind him, the footman hurried to keep up. And Mariah, unaware of the eyes that had measured her so closely, stood her ground beneath the stars, unaware that she had just made a far stronger impression than she knew.

Mariah, still simmering with indignation, folded her arms tightly across her chest.

"No words?" she pressed, her voice quieter now but edged with unmistakable disdain. "I thought as much. Perhaps next time, ladies, you will remember that gossip reveals far more about the speaker than about those you choose to slander. And one never knows who might be listening."

Her words settled over them like a sudden frost. Fans stilled. No one moved. No one spoke. With a final, deliberate glance, cool, unwavering, Mariah turned on her heel and strode away, her skirts sweeping behind her in a silken rush. The cluster of young women remained frozen where they stood, pale and shaken, their earlier bravado dissolved into stunned silence.

As Mariah made her way back toward the garden path, the glow and music of the ballroom drawing closer with every step, a surprising sensation coursed through her, exhilaration. Her heart pounded, but not with embarrassment. Not with regret. She had known cruelty before, whispered judgments, condescension veiled in politeness, the quiet exclusion of those who believed themselves superior. But tonight was different. Tonight, she had answered malice not with tears or retreat, but with composure and truth. She lifted her chin, a faint, wry smile touching her lips. Let London gossip all it wished. She had found her voice at last, and she was no longer afraid to use it.

When Mariah re-entered the ballroom through the great double doors, the warmth of candlelight and the swell of music enveloped her like a silken tide. The earlier chill of the garden melted away, replaced by laughter, movement, and the rich hum of society in full bloom. Nora and Agnes spotted her almost at once and hurried across the floor, their faces bright with genuine relief.

"Mariah! There you are, we've been searching everywhere," Nora exclaimed, clasping her hands warmly.

"I only needed a moment of air," Mariah replied with a reassuring smile. "The night was lovelier than I expected."

From across the room, Lord Haywood's gaze found her. He inclined his head in polite acknowledgment, his expression composed, though his eyes lingered with unmistakable curiosity. That small, unreadable smile, half courtesy, half something else, sent an unwelcome flutter through Mariah's chest before she could stop it. She quickly turned her attention back to the sisters, chiding herself for noticing at all.

Despite the unpleasant encounter outside, the remainder of the evening unfolded far better than she had dared to hope. She conversed with several young gentlemen, some earnest, some amusing, others clearly dazzled by her novelty, but none so overwhelming as she had feared. For the first time that night, she found herself laughing freely, the tension in her shoulders easing with every passing moment.

Most delightful of all was her introduction to Lady Elnora Winston, the spirited young marchioness whose fearless defense of the Haywoods had caught Mariah's attention earlier. Elnora proved every bit as formidable and fascinating as she appeared from afar. Beneath her vibrant beauty and quick wit lay a warmth that drew people in. She spoke with confidence, laughed without restraint, and possessed a keen intelligence sharpened by an unyielding sense of justice.

She confided, with a mischievous grin, that she was newly engaged to the Marquess of Throwley, a circumstance she found highly advantageous.

"Being safely betrothed," Elnora said lightly, "grants one remarkable freedom. No one dares silence a woman who is already claimed."

Mariah laughed, delighted by her candor. In Lady Elnora, she sensed not only a potential friend, but an ally, someone who understood that strength and kindness were not opposites, but companions. And as the music swelled once more and the ballroom shimmered around her, Mariah realized that despite her fears, despite the scrutiny and gossip, this night was beginning to mark something new. Not merely her introduction to society, but her arrival within it.

Later, as they stood near one of the tall windows, Mariah noticed a cluster of familiar faces, the same young ladies whose cruel laughter had echoed through the garden earlier. They had returned to the ballroom, their fans fluttering like nervous butterflies, their expressions carefully arranged into masks of smug composure.

"Lady Elnora," Mariah murmured quietly, inclining her head toward them, "who are those women? And why do they seem so determined to spread misery wherever they go?"

Elnora followed her gaze and released a soft, knowing sigh.

"The ringleader in the center is Miss Susannah Brighton."

Mariah frowned slightly. "I don't believe I know the name."

"Most people would rather forget it," Elnora replied evenly. "Her family once held a marquessate, but scandal destroyed them."

"Scandal?" Mariah echoed.

"The late Marquess of Brighton, her grandfather, was a cruel and vicious man," Elnora explained in a lowered voice. "He was accused of starving his servants and executing several maids on false charges meant to conceal his own crimes. It was Lord Haywood's father, the late Duke of Ashford, who reported him to the Crown. An investigation followed, and the charges were proven."

Mariah gasped softly, her hand rising to her lips.

"How horrible."

"The marquess was stripped of his title and sent to Newgate, where he later died," Elnora continued. "Because it could not be proven how much his son knew, the family was spared complete ruin, but their rank was reduced to that of baron. Their wealth evaporated, their influence collapsed, and their place in society was irrevocably diminished."

Mariah's gaze returned to Miss Brighton, whose laughter now rang a little too loudly.

"And she blames the Haywoods for all of it."

Elnora nodded. "With every breath she draws."

"But if her family has fallen so far," Mariah asked thoughtfully, "how does she still command such attention?"

A wry smile curved Elnora's lips.

"Because she refuses to accept reality. She behaves as though nothing has changed, imperious, entitled, and utterly convinced that she is destined for greatness. The other young women are either too timid or too eager for her approval to challenge her. They imitate her cruelty because it costs them nothing, and because it makes them feel powerful by association."

Mariah's expression hardened, sympathy giving way to quiet resolve.

"How pitiful," she said softly. At that moment, the orchestra struck up a lively country dance, laughter and movement rippling through the ballroom. As couples formed, Mariah's curiosity, and perhaps a touch of mischief, got the better of her. She drifted a little nearer to the group under the pretense of admiring the floral arrangements lining the wall, her posture relaxed, her expression serene. But her ears were sharp. And she listened.

A handsome young viscount approached Miss Brighton and bowed deeply.

"Miss Brighton, may I have the honor of this dance?"

She barely deigned to look at him.

"No, thank you," she replied coolly, her tone dismissive. "I prefer not to exhaust myself so early in the evening."

The viscount's face flushed crimson, his humiliation plain to see. He hesitated, then shifted his weight, searching the room for an escape from the awkward moment. His gaze landed on Mariah and immediately brightened. Without another glance at Miss Brighton, he turned and crossed the floor toward her.

"Lady Mariah," he said warmly, bowing with renewed confidence, "might I claim this dance instead?"

Mariah smiled, gracious and composed. "Of course." She placed her hand in his, allowing him to lead her onto the dance floor as the music swelled. As they joined the other couples, Mariah glanced back only once. Miss Brighton stood rigid, her fan clenched too tightly in her hand, a brittle smile fixed upon her lips. Her eyes, sharp and resentful, followed Mariah with unmistakable disdain.

Mariah looked away, a quiet satisfaction blooming in her chest. She did not laugh aloud, but as the dance began and her partner guided her into the first turn, she allowed herself to smile a small, inward smile. Tonight, she was no longer the girl whispered about behind hedges. Tonight, she was very much seen.

From across the room, Susannah watched Mariah twirl in her partner's arms, the candlelight catching in the folds of her pale blue gown. Her painted smile tightened, the corners of her mouth trembling as irritation bled through her carefully composed façade. Nearby, Agnes, Nora, and Elnora stood together, sharing a quiet moment of amusement, until they noticed Susannah's fixed stare. The levity drained at once.

"Well," Susannah drawled, her voice silken and unhurried, "it appears your brother is quite taken with Lady Mariah." Her eyes drifted, slow, deliberate, toward the young man watching Mariah intently, the implication hanging in the air like a challenge no one dared acknowledge. "Tell me, does she resemble your elder sister in that regard? Fond of appropriating men who belong to others?"

Agnes stiffened, her expression frosting over.

"I beg your pardon?" she said, her voice clipped. Nora's chin lifted, her composure cool and unyielding.

"I believe, Miss Brighton, that you are confusing affection with imagination."

Without waiting for a reply, the sisters turned away together, their shoulders squared, unwilling to grant the insult any further acknowledgment. Elnora, however, did not retreat. She stepped forward, meeting Susannah's glare head-on, her voice even but edged with steel.

"I think you've said quite enough, Susannah."

Susannah scoffed, but Elnora continued, unperturbed.

"Everyone in this room knows you convinced yourself the Marquess of Watford was interested in you. The truth is, he never made you any promises. Lady Thornton didn't steal him, he simply fell in love with her."

Susannah's eyes flashed, her fan snapping shut in her hand.

"You may believe that if it comforts you," she hissed, "but *I* know the truth."

Elnora tilted her head slightly, studying her with frank curiosity.

"Then why," she asked calmly, "do you expend so much energy pursuing Lord Haywood? If you despise his family as fervently as you claim, why seek to marry into it?"

Susannah's composure finally cracked.

"Because I *deserve* to be a duchess," she snapped. "It is the least they owe me after the way his father humiliated my family."

Elnora exhaled slowly, a mix of pity and weariness crossing her features.

"You are truly hopeless, Susannah." With that, she turned away and rejoined Agnes and Nora, leaving Miss Brighton standing alone, fuming in her silks, her pride bruised far more deeply than she would ever admit.

Across the ballroom, Mariah laughed softly as her partner guided her through the final turn of the dance, blissfully unaware that she had just become the unspoken center of a battle she never sought, and one she had already won.

8

Caught Beneath the Chandeliers

Mariah had just rejoined her father and grandmother when the atmosphere of the ballroom subtly shifted. Conversations softened, laughter dipped, and even the musicians seemed to hesitate between sets, as though sensing the change. She felt it before she saw him.

The Duke of Ashford crossed the floor with unhurried confidence, his tall frame drawing instinctive attention. Heads turned. Fans paused mid-flutter. Whispers rippled outward like a tide.

He stopped before her and bowed, precise and elegantly.

"Lady Mariah," he said, his deep voice carrying just far enough to be heard, "would you do me the honor of this dance?"

Her heart gave an unmistakable leap. She looked up to meet his gaze, and something in his eyes, warmth, curiosity, a flicker of unmistakable amusement, made her breath catch. It was as though he knew precisely the effect he had upon her and found it quietly intriguing.

"I—yes, Your Grace," she managed, her cheeks warming despite herself. A faint smile touched his lips, controlled, and devastating. He offered his hand, and when her fingers rested against his palm, a strange steadiness settled over her, even as her pulse raced. The musicians struck up a quadrille, and together they moved toward the floor. As they took their places, Mariah became acutely aware of the attention trained upon them, the weight of curious gazes, the hush of anticipation. This was no ordinary dance. London was watching.

When he placed his hand lightly at her waist, the contact sent a shiver through her, unexpected and electric. His touch was confident but never intrusive, guiding her with an ease that spoke of skill and restraint in equal measure.

"You dance beautifully," he murmured, his voice pitched low, meant for her alone. Mariah allowed herself a small smile.

"You dance well yourself, Your Grace, though I was told you rarely do."

A glimmer of laughter warmed his eyes.

"I only dance," he replied quietly, "when I find a partner worth the effort."

Her breath faltered for just a moment, though she forced herself to maintain composure.

"Then I suppose I should feel honored."

"You should," he said softly, his smile deepening just enough to be dangerous. As the music swelled and they moved in perfect harmony, turning, stepping, gliding as though they had danced together a hundred times before, Mariah felt herself slipping into something unexpected. The chandeliers blurred into starlight, the murmurs of the room faded, and for a brief, breathtaking span of time, there was only the rhythm of the music and the man at her side.

She did not know what the future held, only that this moment, this dance, would linger long after the final note faded. And somewhere deep within her, an undeniable certainty took root: Nothing would ever be quite the same again.

Fury twisted across Susannah Brighton's face the instant she saw the Duke of Ashford dancing with Mariah. Her painted lips parted in stunned disbelief before pressing into a thin, venomous line. One gloved hand clenched around her fan so tightly the ivory ribs creaked in protest. Elnora, ever alert to moments of poetic justice, strolled past her with a languid grace and a knowing smile.

"Well," she said sweetly, pausing just long enough to let the sight sink in, "it appears His Grace has chosen his partner most deliberately this evening."

Susannah did not reply, but the flicker of hatred in her eyes was unmistakable. One of her companions, either braver or far more foolish than the rest, leaned close and whispered, "He certainly seems quite taken with her."

Susannah turned on the girl with a glare sharp enough to draw blood.

"She will not have him," she hissed under her breath, each word coiled with fury. "I will do whatever it takes to make him mine, and she will regret ever daring to stand in my way."

The girl shrank back at once, pale and silent. Elnora, already moving on, caught the final words and allowed herself a quiet, rueful smile. She shook her head almost imperceptibly as she melted back into the crowd.

Hell, hath no fury like a Brighton scorned, she thought wryly, *and heaven help anyone foolish enough to stand in her path.*

Lord Haywood's gaze burned with quiet intensity, and though he spoke little as they danced, Mariah felt it all the same, every measured glance, every unspoken thought. Her breath came faster, her heart pounding in time with the music. She was keenly aware of the eyes upon them, the murmurs and speculation rippling through the ballroom, but it was not the crowd that made her feel unsteady. It was him.

When his hand guided her through the final turn, his touch was confident yet restrained, respectful, deliberate, and utterly disarming. She lowered her gaze, willing herself to breathe, to regain control. His nearness unsettled her in a way she could neither ignore nor fully understand.

This cannot be love, she told herself firmly. *It is nothing more than infatuation. A moment. A reaction to novelty. I still love Oliver. I must.* And yet, as their steps carried them across the floor, warmth bloomed in her chest despite her resolve. Garrett Haywood's charm was not polished flirtation or practiced gallantry. It was quieter than that, rooted in self-possession, steadiness, and an integrity that did not seek attention, yet commanded it all the same.

When the final notes of the quadrille faded, he bowed low over her hand, his lips brushing the air just above her knuckles.

"Thank you, Lady Mariah," he murmured, his voice smooth as velvet.

"The pleasure was mine, Your Grace," she replied softly, though her pulse had yet to steady. He escorted her back to where her father and grandmother stood waiting, his hand lingering for a single, dangerous heartbeat longer than propriety allowed before he released her. That brief contact sent a shiver through her.

Mariah had scarcely drawn a full breath when another gentleman stepped forward, tall, impeccably dressed, and wearing the unmistakable expression of a man thoroughly pleased with himself.

"Lady Mariah," he said with a practiced smile, "may I claim the next dance?"

She recognized him at once, the Marquess of Bromley, Lord Peter Gilmore. From the corner of her eye, she caught Nora and Agnes exchanging a glance and rolling their eyes in perfect, synchronized warning. Their reaction only stirred her curiosity.

"Of course, My Lord," she replied politely, placing her hand in his. Yet even as she turned toward the floor once more, Mariah could not help but glance back, just once, toward the place where Garrett Haywood stood. And she wondered, with equal parts dread and longing, whether the dance she had just shared was the beginning of something she was not yet ready to name.

The Marquess of Bromley proved to be every bit as presumptuous as he was polished. His arm settled around Mariah's waist with a familiarity that skirted the edge of insolence, and more than once she was forced to shift subtly away to maintain a proper distance. His grip never tightened, but neither did it retreat, as though he were testing how much she would tolerate.

"Lady Mariah," he murmured, angling his head closer with an easy confidence that set her teeth on edge, "permit me to say how utterly breathtaking you look this evening. I confess, I am quite smitten already."

Mariah kept her expression serene, though her brows drew together almost imperceptibly.

"Thank you, Lord Gilmore," she replied with measured civility. He chuckled softly and leaned nearer still.

"You say that as though you do not quite believe me."

"I do not doubt your sincerity," she said coolly, meeting his gaze without flinching, "only the frequency with which you must offer such compliments."

For the briefest moment, his grin faltered. Then it returned, broader than before.

"Ah," he said lightly, "a sharp wit to match your beauty. How very dangerous."

Mariah smiled sweetly and offered no further encouragement. The remainder of the dance seemed to stretch endlessly, each measured turn an exercise in patience. When at last the music concluded, Lord Gilmore escorted her back toward her father and grandmother, his hand lingering at her elbow longer than necessary, his reluctance plain. She curtsied with polite finality.

"Thank you for the dance, My Lord."

He hesitated, clearly weighing whether to prolong the moment, but Mariah inclined her head in dismissal and stepped away with brisk grace, leaving him standing alone upon the edge of the floor. Only then did she allow herself a quiet breath of relief.

She found Nora near the edge of the room, standing alone and watching the dancers with mild amusement, one gloved hand resting lightly against the balustrade. Agnes was still engaged in conversation with an older gentleman nearby, nodding politely as he spoke at length about some political matter. Grateful for a moment's refuge, Mariah slipped to Nora's side, relief softening her features.

"That was... an experience," she murmured under her breath. Nora laughed quietly and linked her arm through Mariah's.

"You didn't enjoy dancing with Lord Gilmore?"

"Oh, he dances well enough," Mariah replied with a wry smirk. "But he was dreadfully forward and quite convinced of his own perfection. I cannot imagine why any woman would tolerate him for longer than a single set."

Nora sighed, her amusement fading into something more reflective.

"It's a shame, really. He and my brother were once close friends. They grew up together, inseparable as children."

Mariah blinked in surprise. "Truly? They scarcely acknowledged one another this evening."

"That is because everything changed when our father died and Garrett inherited the dukedom," Nora explained quietly as they began to ascend the grand staircase, the sounds of the ballroom softening behind them.

"Peter Gilmore's envy is... relentless. It began slowly during their adolescent years, but he never forgave Garrett for receiving what he believed should have been his, status, admiration, influence. The friendship withered, and bitterness took its place."

Mariah frowned. "It's not as though your brother had much choice in becoming the new duke. His father died, and he was forced to step into the role. Besides, being a duke isn't merely a title, it's endless responsibility and expectation. Why would anyone envy that?"

Nora gave a small, rueful smile. "Because Lord Gilmore sees only the privileges, never the burdens. In his mind, a duke's life is one of power, wealth at his command, doors opening without effort, and women vying endlessly for his attention."

Mariah shook her head. "Your brother doesn't strike me as the sort who enjoys such nonsense."

"He doesn't," Nora said, a note of pride in her voice. "Garrett despises pretension. But Peter has made a sport of undermining him. Whenever Garrett shows interest in a young lady, Peter swoops in first, flattering, courting, even proposing once or twice, simply to prove that he can."

"How very childish," Mariah muttered. "Perhaps he should turn his attention to Miss Brighton. She seems ambitious enough for two."

Nora's lips twitched before she laughed outright.

"He did once, years ago, before her family's disgrace. But now that her father's rank has been reduced and her reputation tarnished, she's beneath his notice. Peter wants a wife who will elevate him, not remind him of failure."

"Then they deserve one another," Mariah said dryly. "They could spend their lives scheming and stepping on others while the rest of us enjoy a little peace."

Nora smiled at her with open admiration.

"You truly are refreshing, Lady Mariah."

Mariah returned the smile, though her thoughts drifted elsewhere, to Garrett Haywood's steady presence, the quiet intensity in his gaze, the way her heart had betrayed her each time he looked at her. She told herself it was foolish, that a single dance meant nothing. And yet, as the music swelled again below and laughter floated up the staircase, she could not help but wonder, just a little, whether his interest might one day become something far more dangerous than a dance.

A few minutes later, Mariah and Nora descended the corridor together, their earlier gravity softened by shared laughter. They reached the landing and were just about to return to the ballroom when a flushed young baron hurried up the stairs and bowed deeply before Nora.

"Lady Nora, might I have the honor of the next dance?"

Nora's cheeks warmed with polite amusement.

"You may, My Lord."

Mariah watched her friend descend gracefully, sapphire skirts shimmering in the candlelight as she disappeared into the throng below. Left momentarily alone, Mariah exhaled. The press of bodies, the heat, the constant scrutiny, it was all becoming too much. The night air beckoned. She turned toward the quieter corridor leading to the balconies overlooking the gardens, eager for a few stolen moments beneath the stars. But before she could take more than two steps, a voice, deep, slurred, and unmistakable, stopped her cold.

"Well, Lady Mariah," it drawled, thick with drink, "what a pleasure to see you again."

Her blood chilled. Slowly, she lifted her gaze. The Earl of Wyndham stood before her, swaying slightly. His eyes were bloodshot, his complexion ruddy with excess. His cravat hung askew, his coat rumpled, and the sour stench of brandy clung to him like a fog.

"Lord Dalton," she said sharply, straightening. "What are you doing here?"

He grinned crookedly and stepped closer.

"Why, I've come to see you, of course. You've caused me no end of trouble, my dear. Ever since that unfortunate business at Hethersett, Lord Williams and Lord Camden insist on shadowing me as if I were some criminal."

"You are a criminal," Mariah replied icily, "and you deserve to be watched after what you did to your maid. You have no one to blame but yourself. You abuse your servants and disgrace your title."

His face twisted with fury. "My maid wanted to lie with me!" he spat, his voice rising loud enough to turn several heads below.

"Enough!" Mariah hissed, mortified. She stepped back instinctively, but he lunged forward and seized her arm in a bruising grip, hauling her close. The stench of brandy and bitterness assaulted her senses.

From the corner of her eye, she caught movement, Susannah Brighton and her cluster of companions had paused nearby, their expressions gleaming with vicious interest. Below them, she saw Lord Haywood crossing toward his sister Agnes, his posture abruptly alert. Then her father emerged from the ballroom.

The Duke of Kent's gaze swept the staircase, and the instant he saw Dalton's hand clamped around his daughter's arm, his face darkened with cold fury. He surged forward. Before he could reach them, however, the duke's steward appeared at Mariah's side.

"My Lord," Mr. Wellington said firmly, positioning himself between them, "you must leave at once." He gestured sharply, and two footmen stepped forward. Dalton sneered.

"Leave? I'm merely speaking with the lady."

"You are causing a scene," Wellington replied coolly. "And you are intoxicated. These men will escort you out."

The footmen, Howard and Jake, moved in at once, each reaching for one of Dalton's arms. He staggered backward in furious protest, colliding with a servant carrying a tray of crystal glasses. The man wobbled, his breath leaving him in a sharp gasp as he struggled to keep his balance, the glasses chiming in fragile protest.

"Get your hands off me!" Dalton roared, swinging wildly.

When the footmen attempted to restrain him a second time, Dalton lurched forward with reckless force, crashing into the same stunned servant. Unable to recover, the man stumbled helplessly into Mariah. The impact drove her backward, her footing failing beneath her as she fought to remain upright.

Seizing the chaos, the Earl of Wyndham struck. With a sudden, vicious shove, he sent the tray flying upward and outward. Crystal glasses slid, tipped, and then began to rain down upon Mariah.

"Mariah!" her father shouted, rushing forward. Time seemed to slow. The music from the ballroom faded to a distant, distorted hum, as though the world itself had drawn a breath and forgotten how to release it. Mariah's heel slipped on the smooth marble stair, and a sharp cry tore from her throat. She pitched backward, instinctively reaching out, grasping for balance, for fabric, for anything that might stop the fall, while her other hand flew up to shield her head from the cascade of falling glass above.

Then an arm, strong, certain, unyielding, wrapped around her waist. The world tilted, spun, and then steadied all at once as she was pulled firmly against a broad chest. Another hand came up behind her head, cradling it protectively and pressing her face into the shelter of his shoulder as he leaned over her, his body angled deliberately to shield her from the raining shards. The crash of shattering crystal exploded behind them, sharp and violent, followed by gasps and startled cries from every direction.

For one heartbeat... then another... everything went utterly still. Mariah blinked, her breath lodged painfully in her chest, her heart hammering so fiercely she thought it might break free. She was dimly aware of warmth, solid, immovable, holding her upright. Of strength braced around her like a wall against chaos. The scent that surrounded her, fresh linen touched with sandalwood and something darker, warmer beneath it, wrapped around her senses, grounding her even as her limbs trembled.

Slowly, as the shock began to ebb, she lifted her gaze. Lord Haywood's dark eyes met hers, steady and intent, his grip secure but careful, one hand braced protectively at the small of her back. For several suspended heartbeats, neither of them moved nor spoke, the moment stretching thin and electric. Then reality rushed back in. Her father reached them at once, breathless, his face ashen with fear. Agnes and Nora hurried to their brother's side. Hands pressed anxiously to their mouths.

"Mariah, are you all right?" the Duke of Kent demanded, his voice unsteady with fear. Mariah blinked rapidly, the world slowly righting itself as Lord Haywood eased his hold and stepped back, though not before ensuring she was steady on her feet. Her heart still thundered wildly in her chest, the echo of panic slow to fade, but she forced a small, reassuring smile for her father's sake.

"I'm fine, Papa. Truly," she said, drawing a careful breath to steady herself. "Only... startled."

James Kensington searched her face, his gaze sweeping over her as if to reassure himself she was unharmed. Only then did he turn to the man who had intervened so swiftly.

"That was an impressive rescue, Your Grace," he said, gratitude and authority woven together in his tone. Lord Haywood inclined his head slightly, the intensity that had flared moments before settling into something quieter, more controlled.

"I'm only grateful I was close enough to intervene," he replied, his voice calm but sincere.

Mariah lifted her gaze to him once more, still shaken, still keenly aware of how close disaster had come, and acutely aware of the man standing before her. Heat crept into her cheeks as she gathered herself and sank into a small, formal curtsy.

"Thank you, Your Grace," she said softly. "For... catching me."

For a fleeting instant, his eyes lingered on hers, warm, searching, before he stepped back and propriety reclaimed the space between them. Yet the imprint of his touch remained, unmistakable and lingering, long after the danger had passed. A faint smile touched his lips, restrained yet unmistakable.

"It was my honor, Lady Mariah."

Before the moment could deepen into something dangerously intimate, her father pulled her into his arms, his hands firm as he looked her over from head to toe.

"Are you certain you are unharmed?" he asked urgently.

"Yes, Papa," she assured him, her voice gentle but sincere. "I only need a moment to calm my racing heart."

She slipped away, down the corridor, the cool air beyond offering blessed relief. Behind her, the Duke of Kent's voice rang out, cold, precise, and utterly unforgiving.

"Get him out of my house."

Footmen surged forward, seizing Lord Dalton as his drunken protests dissolved into slurred outrage. The murmurs of scandal rippled through the assembled guests as he was dragged from the staircase and down the hall, his disgrace as public as it was deserved.

Mariah did not look back. Her pulse still raced, her skin still tingled where Lord Haywood's arm had held her, but beneath the shock, beneath the fear, something else stirred. And she knew, with sudden, unsettling clarity, that the evening had changed far more than the course of a single dance.

From their vantage near the gallery, Agnes and Nora watched the scene unfold with breathless fascination, scarcely daring to blink. The moment Mariah stumbled, and Garrett caught her, their hearts leapt in unison.

When Elnora slipped up beside them, her sharp eyes taking in everything at once, both sisters turned eagerly toward her, their expressions alight.

"Did you see that?" Agnes whispered, gripping Nora's arm as though to steady herself. "The way Garrett caught her, so instinctive, so *protective*."

Nora nodded fervently, her eyes shining.

"I swear, the tension between them was enough to set the very air ablaze. One more second, and I might have swooned myself."

Elnora smirked, folding her arms with knowing satisfaction.

"Oh, don't faint just yet," she murmured. "If this evening is any indication, sparks like that won't stay hidden for long. Men don't look at women that way without consequence."

The three young women exchanged conspiratorial smiles, delight dancing between them as the orchestra cautiously resumed and the murmur of conversation crept back into the ballroom.

9

Snowfall on the Balcony

Mariah fled down the corridor, her pulse still racing. She knew only that she had to get away, from the ballroom, from the noise, and most of all from Lord Haywood. Every beat of her heart echoed the memory of his arm around her waist, the solid warmth of his body shielding hers, the low timbre of his voice when he spoke her name.

Good heavens, what had just happened? Had it been nothing more than a moment born of chaos, or had he felt it too, that sudden, unmistakable spark that had leapt between them at his touch? She pressed a trembling hand to her chest and quickened her pace. How was she meant to face him again without betraying herself, without blushing like a burning inferno, or worse, swooning like some infatuated schoolgirl?

At the far end of the hall, she pushed open a pair of tall French doors that led onto one of the balconies overlooking the gardens. The night air rushed in, cold and sharp, scented faintly with pine and frost. She stepped outside and drew the doors closed behind her, welcoming the chill as it kissed her flushed cheeks and slowed the frantic rhythm of her thoughts.

For several moments, she did nothing but breathe. In. Out. Slowly. The quiet, wrapped around her like a balm, soothing the storm within. Then, out of the corner of her eye, she noticed a glimmer drifting through the lamplight. A single snowflake floated down and caught in her golden curls. Then another. And another. Her breath caught, and a smile, wide and unguarded, bloomed across her face.

"It's snowing," she whispered, wonder softening her voice. The world seemed to pause as the snowfall thickened, each flake spinning lazily in the gaslight before settling on the stone balustrade. Below, the garden began to shimmer as a delicate white veil spread across the paths and hedges. Mariah laughed quietly, the sound light and breathless, carried away by the wind.

The beauty of it, the stillness, the hush, felt almost sacred. For a fleeting moment, she forgot Lord Dalton's drunken fury, the whispers and stares, her father's fear. All that remained was the soft descent of snow and the faint echo of a waltz drifting from the ballroom behind her.

Without realizing it, she began to move. Her feet glided lightly across the marble balcony, skirts whispering as she turned, her body following the distant rhythm of the music. She closed her eyes and let herself spin beneath the falling snow, the cold air and melody carrying her away.

For the first time that evening, perhaps for the first time in a very long while, Mariah felt utterly, exquisitely free.

Suddenly, strong hands seized her waist. Mariah froze, a startled gasp tearing from her throat as she was spun abruptly, forced into a dance she had not chosen, one rough and unbalanced, its intent unmistakable.

"Lord Gilmore!" she exclaimed, recognition striking as the moonlight caught his face. "What are you doing? Release me at once."

He grinned, the smug curve of his mouth catching the pale glow of the lanterns.

"You looked lonely out here," he drawled, guiding her through a slow, deliberate turn that felt less like a dance and more like possession—entirely inappropriate. "I thought I might offer some comfort."

Her eyes flashed. "This is highly improper, my lord. Let go of me. Now."

Instead, his grip tightened, pulling her closer, close enough that she could smell the wine on his breath.

"I merely wished to be certain you weren't hurt," he said silkily. "That little mishap on the stairs must have been quite the shock."

"Yes, it was," she snapped, bracing her hands against his chest in an effort to push away, "and you are not improving matters by laying hands on me."

He chuckled softly, then leaned closer, lowering his voice.

"I asked your father for your hand in marriage."

The words struck like a slap.

"You—what?" she demanded, disbelief stealing her breath.

"Just before the ball," he continued, clearly pleased with himself. "The duke told me the decision was yours to make. So here I am, seeking your answer."

Her stomach turned cold. "Then hear it plainly," she said, her voice trembling not with fear but fury. "No. I will not marry you, Lord Gilmore. Your conduct is disgraceful. No decent man, no gentleman, would behave in this manner."

His grin widened, eyes darkening. "Who said I was a gentleman?" He leaned closer still, the predatory gleam in his gaze sending a sharp jolt of fear through her. She twisted again, shoving at his shoulders.

"If you do not release me immediately," she warned, "I will scream and summon help."

He laughed under his breath. "Go on. Cry out. You'll only invite scandal upon yourself. Imagine how swiftly London will feast on the tale, how your father's joy at reclaiming you will sour into shame."

"You are vile," she hissed, struggling harder now.

"Perhaps," he murmured, his lips angling toward hers, "but I always get what I want."

Before he could close the final distance between their lips, a blur of motion erupted from the shadows. A fist connected with a sharp crack. Lord Gilmore staggered backward, clutching his jaw, shock and pain flashing across his face as snowflakes scattered at his feet. Mariah cried out and stumbled back, her heart pounding violently as she pressed against the stone balustrade. Between her and her assailant stood Lord Haywood.

His chest rose and fell with restrained fury, his hand still clenched from the blow. Snow dusted his dark hair and shoulders, lending him the aspect of something elemental and unyielding.

"Touch her again," he said quietly, his voice low and lethal, "and I will do far more than bruise your jaw."

The snow fell silently between them, the night suspended in breathless stillness. Mariah's pulse refused to steady. Her rescuer, again, stood like a storm before her, radiating a controlled wrath that made her feel both shaken and profoundly safe. And at that moment, she could no longer pretend what stirred within her was mere infatuation. Whatever bound her to Garrett Haywood now was far deeper, and far more dangerous, than she had ever expected.

Lord Gilmore staggered upright, blood streaking from his nose. Fury and humiliation warred across his features as he wiped at the crimson smear with the back of his hand.

"What the devil do you think you're doing, Haywood?" he snarled, his words slurred yet venomous. "Can't stomach that a young lady prefers me to you?"

Before Mariah could voice her outrage at the arrogant presumption, Lord Haywood was already moving. In one swift, decisive motion, he seized Gilmore by the front of his waistcoat and hauled him forward. His grip was ironclad, his posture unyielding, and when he spoke, his voice was low, controlled and lethal.

"The lady," he said evenly, every syllable controlled, "made herself perfectly clear. She did not welcome your attention. To ignore a woman's wishes and lay hands on her uninvited is not the act of a gentleman, it is the act of a coward and a rake."

Mariah's breath caught. There was no need for raised voices. The quiet authority in his tone, restrained yet seething, carried far more menace than any shout. Gilmore's jaw tightened, his pride stung raw.

"Coward, am I?" he spat, and swung. Mariah didn't think. Instinct surged ahead of fear. She darted between them, arms outstretched, her heart hammering.

"Stop!"

The movement startled them, both, and nearly cost her dearly. Lord Haywood reacted faster than thought. His hand shot out, catching Gilmore's fist inches from her face. The force of the blow trembled through his grip as he twisted Gilmore's arm away. Gilmore wrenched free with a curse, his face flushed with rage and disbelief.

"Are you mad?" he barked at Mariah. "Stepping between fighting men? This is none of your concern!"

"Oh, really?" Mariah snapped, fear giving way to fury. Her voice rang clear and unyielding. "You claimed I was interested in you, yet it was *you* who pursued *me*. You tried to compromise me twice this evening, and His Grace merely intervened to protect my dignity. You ought to be ashamed, Lord Gilmore."

He let out a harsh, humorless laugh.

"I see how it is. It's his title that caught your fancy, isn't it? You'd hardly spare him a glance otherwise."

That was the final insult. Mariah drew herself up to her full height, her eyes blazing.

"You know nothing of women, and certainly nothing of me," she said, her voice trembling with righteous fury. "A title is meaningless when the man behind it is cruel, arrogant, and without honor. Kindness, courage, humor, and decency are what make a man worthy of admiration, qualities you seem to lack entirely."

Gilmore's smirk faltered beneath her unflinching gaze. Still breathless, she went on.

"If you ever hope to impress a lady, I suggest you begin by learning how to respect one. Now, if you will excuse me, I bid you good evening."

She turned to leave, but before she could take a step, Lord Haywood's hand closed gently around her arm, drawing her behind him. A heartbeat later, Gilmore lunged forward, his hand outstretched as though to seize her again. He never reached her.

The balcony doors burst open, and Mr. Wellington strode out, with two footmen flanking him, his expression carved from iron, but Peter Gilmore paid no intention to them. His fury was on Mariah.

"You are a foolish woman, or perhaps far more calculating than I first believed," he sneered, his lip curling. "I wondered how you rose so quickly in Haywood's favor. Tell me, are you, his strumpet? Is that why you cling to his arm so boldly, why he leaps to your defense at every opportunity?" His eyes raked over her with deliberate insult.

"Or is it ambition that drives you? A pretty face, eager manners, and a talent for ensnaring men of rank, hardly uncommon, after all. You were raised as the daughter of a viscount, and discovering yourself to be the true daughter of a duke must have gone to your head. Of course, you would do anything to avoid returning to such a low station."

Mariah gasped, mortified, heat flooding her cheeks as the weight of his words struck like a blow. Then, before she could restrain herself, she struck him. The sharp crack of her palm against his cheek rang out, stunning the surrounding air into silence.

Lord Haywood surged forward at once, seizing him again, but that was when her father's steward stepped in.

"I believe that will be quite enough, Lord Gilmore," he said coolly, his voice carrying unmistakable authority. "Let me remind you whose daughter you are addressing. Your conduct tonight is unworthy of your title and disgraceful in every sense."

Gilmore glowered, but one glance at the two burly footmen was enough to drain the defiance from his eyes. With a muttered curse, he allowed himself to be escorted away, his wounded pride far more visible than the blood still marking his face.

As the doors closed behind them, silence settled over the balcony once more. Snowflakes drifted lazily through the open archway, melting as they touched the cold marble floor. For a moment, neither of them spoke. Lord Haywood turned back to Mariah, his voice noticeably gentler now.

"Are you hurt?"

She looked up at him, and the concern in his brown eyes nearly undid her. It was not the sharp vigilance of moments before, but something quieter, protective, sincere.

"No," she said softly. "Just... shaken." She drew a breath. "Thank you for stepping in."

He exhaled slowly, running a hand through his dark hair.

"Gilmore is a cad," he said grimly. "I'm sorry you were forced to endure that."

"He frightened me at first, and his insults cut deep," Mariah admitted, her voice low. "But anger quickly took his place. I cannot abide men who use their strength or hurt feelings to humiliate others."

A faint, rueful smile touched his lips.

"You're braver than most men I know."

She let out a small, nervous laugh, then her gaze fell to his hand. A thin line of crimson glistened across his knuckles, catching the pale glow of the lantern light.

"You're bleeding, Your Grace."

He glanced down, unconcerned. "It's nothing."

"Please," she said quickly, stepping closer. "Let me tend to it." Her gloved fingers trembled as she drew a handkerchief from the pocket of her gown and pressed it gently to the wound. The distance between them shrank with every breath. Lord Haywood's eyes softened as he watched her, his earlier fury replaced by something quieter, something far more dangerous to her heart.

When the bleeding slowed, she lifted her gaze and found him studying her face. His expression was unreadable, yet there was a warmth there that made her pulse flutter wildly.

"There," she whispered, stepping back. "That should suffice, for now."

He nodded once, though he did not immediately move away.

"Thank you, Lady Mariah," he murmured. Then, with deliberate care, he lifted her hand and brushed his lips across the fabric of her glove. The world tilted. Her pulse thundered in her ears. The cold air, the faint scent of his cologne, the warmth of his touch, everything blurred into one breathless moment.

"Your Grace..."

They both turned. A young servant stood awkwardly in the doorway, cheeks crimson. "Forgive me for interrupting, but... your mother wishes to speak with you."

Lord Haywood cleared his throat and released Mariah's hand.

"Of course," he said, bowing lightly. "Good night, Lady Mariah."

"Good night, Your Grace," she replied, her voice softer than she intended.

As he disappeared inside, she pressed her fingers lightly to her palm, as though she might capture the lingering warmth of his lips. Twice now he had come to her rescue. Twice he had seen her at her most vulnerable, and yet she had never felt so fiercely alive. Uncertain what to do with herself, Mariah returned indoors, her heart still racing. The corridor was quiet now, the laughter and music from the ballroom distant and muffled. She had nearly reached the grand staircase when a faint sound reached her ears, a woman's muffled sob.

She slowed, listening. The sound came again, unmistakable this time. Curiosity and concern warred within her. Turning toward the sound, she followed it down the corridor until she reached a small washroom, its door slightly ajar. Voices murmured softly inside, low and urgent, attempting to comfort someone in distress. Mariah paused just outside, her hand hovering over the latch. Taking a steadying breath, she wondered what new heartbreak, or secret, the night still held in store before gently stepping closer.

"Why would he say he intends to marry me if he has no intention of doing so?" a young woman sobbed, her voice breaking between words. "He even promised my father, promised him, on his deathbed, that he would propose soon."

A sympathetic voice replied softly, "Men are unpredictable, dearest. They make vows when caught in sentiment and forget them the moment their hearts, or their fancies, shift. Try not to place blame upon Lady Mariah. She likely has no knowledge of any promises made to you."

"I wouldn't be so sure about that," came a sharp, cutting tone that made Mariah's stomach twist. Susannah. Of course. Mariah's fingers tightened against the edge of the doorframe, her pulse quickening as recognition settled like ice in her veins.

"I saw her and Lord Haywood together on the balcony only minutes ago," Susannah continued, her voice smooth and venomous, each word delivered with deliberate precision. "They looked quite... cozy, if you ask me."

A ripple of shocked gasps swept through the room, silks rustling as the women turned toward her.

"Whatever do you mean?" one asked breathlessly. Susannah lifted a delicate shoulder in an artful shrug.

"Oh, come now, you must have noticed. Lady Mariah seems to require rescuing at every possible opportunity. Convenient, is it not? Twice tonight she has been 'saved' by Lord Haywood himself." She gave a soft, knowing laugh. "The first time from that drunken man, whom I suspect she may even have paid to cause a scene."

"Paid him?" another woman whispered, horror edging her voice.

"Yes," Susannah replied calmly, savoring the stunned silence that followed. "And afterward, she lured Lord Gilmore onto the balcony. He tried to kiss her, of course, men like him always do, and once again, His Grace appeared at precisely the right moment to play the gallant hero."

A chorus of shocked murmurs followed, swelling with disbelief and indignation. The weeping girl broke into open sobs, her grief echoing off the tiled walls.

"Was that really necessary, Susannah?" another voice snapped, sharp with anger. "Esther is already heartbroken. Must you twist the knife further?"

"So?" Susannah answered coolly. "Better she knows the truth now than continue believing in a man who so clearly prefers another."

"You are impossible," the same woman retorted. "You speak this way only because jealousy consumes you. Everyone knows it. Lord Haywood will never marry you, and your spite makes you pitiable."

Susannah laughed softly, a sound devoid of warmth.

"Believe what you wish. But if His Grace can so easily abandon one woman for another, then perhaps none of us should waste our hopes on him."

A hesitant voice broke in. "Perhaps... perhaps we should make their little meeting public. The ton ought to know what sort of woman Lady Mariah truly is."

"Oh, do be sensible," the sharper woman countered. "If you spread such nonsense, it will only force him to marry her, and that will not bring him back to Esther."

Susannah's smile sharpened, her eyes glittering with cold satisfaction.

"Perhaps not," she said icily. "But at least it would ruin her."

Just beyond the door, Mariah stood frozen, every word striking her like a physical blow. Her pulse thundered in her ears, drowning out the distant strains of music as the full weight of their cruelty settled upon her shoulders. The glittering ballroom behind her, the chandeliers, the laughter, the polished smiles, felt suddenly unreal, as though she had been cast adrift from it all.

In that fragile, suspended moment, she understood with chilling clarity just how merciless London society could be. Polite words could wound as deeply as blades, and reputation was a weapon wielded without mercy. If she wished to endure, if she wished to claim her place and protect what little she held dear, she would have to fight. And she would have to do so with strength, resolve, and a heart steeled against cruelty.

Mariah had heard enough. Her pulse thundered in her ears as she stepped back from the door, every cruel word echoing through her mind. The corridor felt suddenly too narrow, the air thick and suffocating. She turned and fled, down the hallway, up the stairs, her slippers barely touching the carpet as she ran blindly toward the only place that felt safe. Her bedchamber.

Once inside, she shut the door and leaned against it, pressing her back to the cool wood as though it were the only thing holding her upright. Her hands trembled violently. Her chest ached with each breath she dragged into her lungs. Tears burned fiercely behind her eyes, but she clenched her jaw and refused to let them fall.

"Of course," she whispered bitterly into the silence. "Of course it was all a charade." Her thoughts raced, tumbling over one another in cruel clarity. How perfectly it all fit, his timely appearances, his gallantry, the way he had looked at her as though she were something precious. A performance. A means to an end. He had used her, used her to provoke jealousy, to free himself from a promise he had never intended to keep.

Humiliation scorched her cheeks as anger coiled tight around her heart.

"How could I have been so foolish?" she murmured, pacing the room like a caged thing. "So easily taken in by a charming smile and heroic gestures?"

She clenched her fists. Nails biting into her palms as though pain might anchor her. No. She would not allow herself to be played. Not again. Not after the betrayal she had endured. And yet, a traitorous whisper rose unbidden in her mind. *He didn't seem false.* Mariah stopped short, squeezing her eyes shut as though she might crush the thought out of existence.

"No," she said aloud, her voice shaking. "I will not be naïve." She forced herself to breathe, to think. Her gaze drifted toward the window, where snowflakes continued to fall softly, brushing against the glass like fragile promises. Images surfaced against her will, Nora's laughter, Agnes's kindness, the warmth with which his family had welcomed her. Those women had not been acting. Of that, she was certain.

"They wouldn't deceive me," she whispered, softer now. "They couldn't." Her hands curled at her sides, resolve stiffening her spine. "I won't let this poison what we've begun," she said firmly, swiping at the tears that had finally escaped. "I won't."

But conviction could not mend a wounded heart. She crossed the room and extinguished the lamp, plunging the chamber into shadow. When she sank onto the edge of her bed, the strength left her all at once. The ache in her chest pulsed dully, relentless and deep. No matter how fiercely she tried to deny it, no matter how harshly she judged herself, one truth refused to be silenced, she was already in love with the man she had just sworn to despise.

10

Caught in His Arms

Over the next several days, Mariah did her utmost to avoid the Duke of Ashford, but such efforts proved nearly impossible. The Kensingtons and the Haywoods moved within the same intimate social orbit, bound by long-standing friendship, shared obligations, and a closeness that predated her arrival in London.

At dinners, carriage rides, and afternoon calls, Mariah found herself surrounded by easy laughter and gracious conversation, warmth she could scarcely bring herself to return. Her cousins spoke of the young duke with fond admiration, praising his intelligence, his dry humor, and his sense of duty. Her father and grandmother regarded him with unmistakable esteem, welcoming his presence as naturally as one would a trusted member of the family. And Garrett Haywood himself gave her no cause for offense.

He was attentive without being intrusive, kind without expectation, unfailingly respectful. Never once did he seek her out alone. Never once did he press for conversation or linger where propriety might be questioned. When their gazes met, his expression was open and courteous, if anything, slightly guarded, as though he, too, walked a careful line. It left her torn and bewildered.

This man bore little resemblance to the one Susannah Brighton had painted with her poison words. There was no arrogance in him, no careless charm wielded to wound another woman's heart. And yet, the memory of those whispers, sharp, deliberate, cruel, clung to Mariah, like a shadow she could not quite dispel. Had everything she felt that night truly been imagined? A moment mistaken for meaning? Or had she been foolish enough to believe in something he never intended to offer?

The uncertainty gnawed at her. And no matter how diligently she tried to distance herself, one truth became increasingly impossible to ignore: If Garrett Haywood had never cared for her at all, then the pain of that realization cut far deeper than pride alone should allow. Which meant her heart, traitorous and tender, had already chosen its side, whether she wished it to.

The day before their planned departure from London, Mariah was summoned to the sitting room. Expecting nothing more than a minor family matter, she entered and stopped short.

"Father—" The word slipped from her lips before she could stop it. She caught herself at once, her breath faltering. "I mean... Lord Winter. What are you doing here?"

The Viscount of Hethersett rose slowly from his chair. He looked older than she remembered, thinner, stooped in a way that spoke of sleepless nights and heavy regret. Yet when his eyes met hers, they shone with the same familiar warmth, now edged with sorrow. Before she could gather herself, her true father stepped forward and placed a steady, reassuring arm around her shoulders.

"I invited Lord Winter, my dear," the Duke of Kent said gently. "It seemed only right. He raised you with love, even under difficult circumstances. I thought it time old wounds were laid to rest."

Mariah swallowed hard as the two men regarded one another, so different in station, yet bound forever by the same child.

"Your Grace," Lord Winter said, bowing deeply, his voice unsteady. "I am profoundly grateful for your kindness, more than I can properly express. And..." He turned to Mariah, emotion tightening his throat.

"Forgive me, my dear child, for failing you. I allowed pride and desperation to blind me. I should have told you the truth long ago, instead of clinging to silence for fear of losing the little I had left."

Mariah's chest, constricted. "And I should not have fled without saying goodbye," she said softly. "I was afraid—afraid you would be angry."

He shook his head, a faint, broken smile touching his lips.

"Not angry, Mariah. Never angry. Only heartbroken. You were my daughter in every way that mattered. I should have been the one to bring you home, to your real father."

Silence settled between them, thick with unspoken years. At last, Lord Winter drew a breath and added quietly, "Your father has paid my debts in full. His generosity has given me the chance to begin again, though I scarcely deserve such mercy."

The Duke of Kent spoke then, his voice calm and dignified.

"You cared for my daughter when I could not. You loved and protected her as your own. Though your final choices were regrettable, they do not erase the good you have done. For that, you have my gratitude, and my forgiveness. You were deceived as well, betrayed by the woman who stole Mariah from me. When you learned the truth, that pain must have cut deeply. I will not hold her crimes against you."

Mariah blinked rapidly as tears threatened. The grace her father showed filled her with awe, and fierce pride. Lord Winter bowed his head, overcome.

"You honor me, Your Grace." Then he turned back to Mariah, his expression tightening with concern. "Before I take my leave, there is something you must know. The Earl of Wyndham, Lord Dalton, is furious with you. He blames you for taking his maid and for drawing attention to his cruelty. The Earl of Norwich and the Marquess of Pedham have begun investigating him, and they've discovered enough to strip him of most of his household. He may even lose his title."

Mariah's eyes widened. "He already caused a dreadful scene at the ball," she said quickly. "He was intoxicated, belligerent. Papa had him removed from the house."

Lord Winter exchanged a grave look with the Duke of Kent.

"That humiliation may have only worsened matters. Dalton does not forgive insult or exposure. He is cornered now, and desperate men are dangerous. I fear he may seek revenge."

A chill crept along Mariah's spine.

"I will be careful," she promised earnestly. "I won't go anywhere alone."

"See that you don't," Lord Winter urged. "Take someone with you always. Lord Dalton is not a man to underestimate."

Mariah nodded solemnly. "Thank you, for the warning. And... for everything."

As Lord Winter prepared to take his leave, Mariah realized something with quiet clarity: though her life had been divided by secrets and lies, she had been loved, truly loved, by two fathers in two very different ways. And now, with one chapter closing and another opening, she sensed that danger still lingered in the shadows, watching, waiting. The past, it seemed, was not quite finished with her yet.

The following morning, the family departed London for Ashford, so that Mariah might at last meet her mother's parents. The journey was long but pleasant, the carriage rolling through countryside dusted with frost, fields and hedgerows glittering as winter quietly claimed the land. Ashford itself, with its rolling hills, winding lanes, and bustling village, proved far lovelier than Mariah had imagined. Stone cottages clustered around the green, smoke curling from chimneys, and the air carried the clean, bracing scent of cold earth and woodsmoke. It felt alive, grounded, and welcoming in a way London never quite had.

Her grandparents greeted her with open arms, their joy unrestrained and unmistakable. Her grandmother wept openly as she held her, murmuring blessings and prayers of gratitude, while her grandfather embraced her with quiet pride before insisting, more than once, that she was the very image of her mother.

Within hours, Mariah found herself swept into a boisterous gathering of aunts, uncles, and cousins she had never known existed. After growing up nearly alone, with only Lord Winter and his brother as family, the noise, laughter, and constant motion overwhelmed her in the best possible way. Voices overlapped, questions came from every direction, and no one seemed willing to let her sit unnoticed for more than a moment.

Her grandmother fussed over her endlessly, straightening her shawl and pressing warm cups of tea into her hands. Her grandfather proudly introduced her to every neighbor within calling distance, proclaiming her return as though it were a village holiday. Her cousins clamored for her attention, eager to hear stories of London, Norwich, and the life she had lived before finding them.

Yet amid the joyful chaos, it was Agnes and Nora Haywood who claimed her time most often. Their easy laughter, gentle teasing, and quiet understanding felt like a refuge. With them, Mariah could breathe, could simply be herself without expectation or scrutiny. Their sisterly companionship was a balm to her heart, steady and reassuring.

Ashford itself charmed her at every turn. Cobbled streets wound past tidy stone houses, and small shops displayed goods in frost-rimmed windows. She was surprised to learn that so many noble families made their homes there, drawn by its beauty and sense of community. That delight, however, was dimmed when she learned that Susannah Brighton, and several of her spiteful companions, were among the residents.

Mariah felt a faint tightening in her chest. It seemed that trouble, like gossip, had a way of traveling wherever it pleased. Even so, as she stood beside Agnes and Nora beneath the pale winter sky, listening to the sounds of a town settling into evening, Mariah reminded herself that this place held far more promise than peril. And this time, she would not face it alone.

The final event of Ashford's fall season was the grand December ball at the Haywood estate, a glittering occasion spoken of weeks in advance by every family in town. The excitement was palpable. Young ladies whispered of it in milliners' shops and confectioners'

parlors, each determined to outshine the rest in gowns, jewels, and charm.

For Mariah, it would be her first true introduction to the social world of Ashford. Nora and Agnes, eager to ensure their new friend made a dazzling impression, insisted on taking her shopping.

The morning proved delightful, filled with laughter, teasing, and sisterly camaraderie, until fate placed them directly in the path of trouble. As the three ladies stepped into the finest dressmaker's shop in town, the lighthearted atmosphere evaporated. Susannah Brighton stood before them, flanked by three companions, one of whom Mariah instantly recognized as the young woman she had overheard weeping over Lord Haywood.

"Lady Mariah," Susannah said coolly, dipping into a shallow curtsy. Her tone was laced with false sweetness, her eyes glittering with disdain. Her friends followed suit, each wearing that smile reserved for polite enemies.

"Miss Brighton," Mariah replied with equal civility, inclining her head in acknowledgment.

"What brings you to Ashford?" Susannah asked, her voice light but her expression sharp as glass. "I was under the impression your father resided in Kent."

"He does," Mariah answered calmly, "but my mother's family is from Ashford, and my father also keeps a small estate nearby."

"Of course he does," Susannah muttered under her breath, her jaw tightening as jealousy flared in her eyes. Another young lady, perhaps emboldened by Susannah's boldness, stepped forward.

"Does that mean your visit is merely to meet relatives, Lady Mariah?"

"Mostly," Mariah said with a polite smile. Before the conversation could sour further, Nora slipped an arm through hers.

"She's also here to attend our family's ball," Nora said cheerfully. "We told her it's the event of the year in Ashford, and we wouldn't hear of her missing it."

Mariah saw at once how Susannah's expression darkened. Her lips thinned. Her eyes narrowed with something between envy and rage. The young lady beside her, Esther, still pale with heartbreak, turned away, blinking back tears. Agnes, sensing the tension, took her sister's arm and guided her toward the display of new gowns, leaving Mariah momentarily alone.

That was all the opportunity Susannah needed. She stepped closer, her voice dropping to a venomous whisper.

"Have you come to gloat, Lady Mariah? To flaunt that Lord Haywood has taken a fancy to you?"

Mariah's spine straightened. Her pulse quickened, but her expression remained composed.

"Whatever makes you think His Grace has taken an interest in me?"

Susannah gave a soft, derisive laugh. "Don't insult my intelligence. You must be quite pleased with yourself, that the Duke of Ashford noticed you the very night you returned to London. You've been parading your newfound importance ever since. Look at poor Esther, she's been inconsolable because of you."

"As if you care about Miss Esther's feelings," Mariah said quietly but firmly, unable to keep her irritation at bay. "And why, pray tell, do you think she is heartbroken on my account?"

"Because since your arrival, you've done everything in your power to ensnare Lord Haywood's affections," Susannah snapped, her composure fraying.

Mariah's eyes flashed. "Whatever are you talking about?"

"Do you truly believe the ton is not talking?" Susannah's voice rose slightly, drawing curious glances from nearby patrons. "Everyone knows you returned to your father's side the very night he was dining with His Grace. Why could you not wait until the following day, unless, of course, you wished to impress him? You used your 'reunion' to gain entry to Ashford's finest circle. How convenient."

It took every ounce of Mariah's restraint not to retaliate with sharp words. Her cheeks burned, but her posture remained regal.

"I assure you, Miss Brighton," she said with icy precision, "I had never even met His Grace before that evening."

Susannah's smile turned cruel as she leaned closer, lowering her voice.

"Oh, I think we both know that isn't entirely true. You stayed overnight at the Haywood residence, didn't you? You two seem rather 'familiar' with each other. And I've seen the way he looks at you. Clearly, he sees you as a woman who knows how to lure a man into her—"

"That is quite enough." Mariah's voice cut through the air like a whip. Several customers turned to stare. Even the shopkeeper froze mid-measure. "Let me remind you who you are addressing, *Miss* Brighton," Mariah continued, her tone calm but fierce. "Your accusations and insinuations are not only false, they are vulgar. I am well aware that you have made yourself known as society's most prolific gossip, but that does not grant you the right to defame others."

Susannah's mouth fell open in shock, her face reddening with fury.

"I pity you," Mariah went on, her voice softening but not wavering. "I truly do. You twist others' happiness into bitterness because you cannot bear to see anyone admired where you are not. I am sorry Miss Esther has not received the proposal she hoped for, but that has nothing to do with me. If you must vent your frustrations, perhaps you should take them up with His Grace himself, if you dare. Though I suspect you prefer to strike from the shadows, like the backbiting coward you are."

A collective gasp swept through the shop. Susannah's friends looked mortified, and even Nora, standing at the counter, gaped at Mariah's boldness. Susannah's face blanched, then flushed a deep crimson.

"How dare you—" she began. But Mariah was already turning away, her chin lifted, her composure unshaken.

"Good day, Miss Brighton."

Although Nora and Agnes had not caught every word exchanged in the dressmaker's shop, they had heard enough of Mariah's cutting retort to know that something dreadful had been said. They hurried after her, their skirts swishing over the snowy cobblestones. Before they reached the waiting carriage, Nora caught her friend gently by the arm.

"Mariah," she said softly, her brow furrowed with concern. "What did Susannah say to provoke you so? I have never seen you look so furious. She must have been completely out of line."

Mariah drew a deep breath through gritted teeth, trying to steady herself.

"She was worse than out of line. She accused me of dreadful things, vile, unthinkable things. She attacked not only my character, but my virtue."

Both sisters gasped in horror.

"Oh, that wretched woman!" Agnes cried, her eyes flashing. "How dare she? She has done this before, spreading poisonous lies whenever jealousy eats at her."

Nora nodded grimly. "She said cruel things about our elder sister as well, after setting her sights on the Marquess of Watford. When he showed no interest, she began whispering scandalous rumors about him and our sister, Lady Thornton. It was horrid."

Agnes sighed. "We kept it from our brother and Mama for as long as we could. Had Garrett learned of it, I dare say he would have called her out in front of all London. Mama would have been heartbroken."

Mariah pressed her lips together, the fire of her anger ebbing into weariness.

"Then perhaps I should not have let her provoke me. But there are limits to what a lady can endure in silence."

Nora squeezed her hand affectionately.

"You did right, Mariah. That woman thrives on others' fear of her tongue. You gave her the truth, and I, for one, am quite proud of you."

After that encounter, however, Mariah's excitement for the Haywood ball waned considerably. The thought of facing Susannah Brighton again filled her with distaste. More than once, she considered sending her regrets, claiming a headache or lingering fatigue from travel. But her father had spoken with such anticipation about the event, her cousins were eager to see her properly presented, and Nora and Agnes had both promised it would be a night to remember. Reluctantly, she agreed to attend.

On the evening of the ball, Martha outdid herself. With patient hands and an artist's precision, she arranged Mariah's thick curls into a graceful coiffure, adorning them with small rose-colored ribbons and pearl pins that gleamed softly beneath the candlelight. Her gown, pale rose silk embroidered with silver leaves along the hem, was breathtaking. It shimmered as she moved, the light catching the delicate threads like morning dew upon petals. Martha clasped her hands together in delight.

"My Lady," she declared proudly, "you'll be the queen of the ball, that's certain."

Mariah smiled faintly at the sentiment, though her heart, beat faster than she liked.

If only I could be invisible instead.

The carriage wheels crunched softly over the snow as they arrived at Conningbrook Hall. The grand estate rose before them, its towers and windows aglow with golden light reflected in the still waters of Conningbrook Lake. The air was crisp, and snowflakes drifted lazily down from a clouded sky. It was a scene of pure enchantment.

As Mariah stepped out beside her father, she drew her shawl tighter around her shoulders. Laughter and music spilled from the great hall and carried across the courtyard, mingling with the faint jingle of sleigh bells and the fresh scent of pine from the garlands framing the entrance. Inside, the air was warm and fragrant with evergreens and polished wood. Candles blazed in crystal sconces, and chandeliers sparkled overhead like constellations brought to life.

The Duke of Ashford greeted them at once, impeccably dressed in black and ivory. His smile was courteous, charming, even, but when his gaze met Mariah's, it lingered for a moment too long. Her pulse quickened, and she lowered her eyes, unable to ignore the warmth that crept into her cheeks.

Before she could recover, the dowager duchess swept forward, exclaiming, "My dear girl, how radiant you look," and pulled Mariah into a fond embrace before she had time to curtsy. Mariah laughed softly, her earlier tension melting away. There was something deeply comforting in the duchess's maternal warmth, and she found herself grateful for the woman's kindness.

Nora and Agnes soon appeared at her side, introducing her to several young ladies gathered nearby, most of them daughters of local gentry or minor noble families. They were bright, cheerful, and refreshingly unpretentious. Mariah felt herself relax among them, grateful for the easy conversation and shared laughter. For the first time in days, she allowed herself to breathe. Perhaps, she thought, this evening would not be as dreadful as she had feared.

Mariah and Nora stood arm in arm near one of the great marble columns as the dowager duchess and her son stepped forward to welcome their guests. Glittering chandeliers bathed the ballroom in golden light, and a hum of anticipation rippled through the crowd. When the orchestra struck its first note, the Duke of Ashford, tall, composed, and striking in his dark attire, lifted his gaze and swept it across the room. For a moment, his eyes searched the assembled guests. Then they found her.

Mariah's heart stuttered. Without hesitation, he crossed the ballroom floor, his stride purposeful, yet unhurried, until he stood before her. His bow was deep and graceful, his voice warm as he spoke.

"Lady Mariah," he said, offering a smile that seemed to still every whispered conversation around them. "Would you do me the honor of the first dance?" He extended his hand, palm open and steady, waiting for her answer.

For a heartbeat, she forgot to breathe. His expression was softer than she remembered, gentle even, and she realized with a start that his eyes were the same deep brown as Agnes's, warm and kind. The resemblance tightened something unexpectedly in her chest. Part of her longed to decline, to retreat into the safety of the crowd. But the weight of her father's and the duchess's approving gazes pressed upon her. Refusal would have been unthinkably rude. She drew a steadying breath, schooling her features into a polite smile.

"It would be my honor, Your Grace."

He bowed again, a flicker of satisfaction glinting behind his eyes as she laid her gloved hand atop his. The warmth of his touch was immediate and utterly disarming.

11

The Promise She Believed

The orchestra began a graceful waltz. The duke guided her onto the dance floor, his hand settling lightly at her waist. She curtsied. He bowed. Then, as the music swelled, they began to move. Mariah tried to maintain her composure, but Lord Haywood's presence unsettled her in ways she could not explain. His movements were smooth, precise, and utterly confident, yet his tone when he spoke, was disarmingly kind. He asked about her childhood in Norwich, her love of riding, the quiet beauty of the countryside. To her surprise, he claimed to share her fondness for solitude and nature. Each word he spoke seemed to draw her deeper into conversation, unraveling the defenses she had so carefully built since her introduction to society.

Who was the real Lord Haywood? she wondered. The charming gentleman who smiled so easily, or the inscrutable man whose reputation had been whispered about all over London?

The waltz came to an end, but before she could retreat, the musicians struck up a lively country dance. Laughter filled the air as couples eagerly joined in, and Lord Haywood, his eyes alight with a hint of mischief, kept hold of her hand.

"One more, Lady Mariah?" he asked softly. She nodded before she could think better of it. The rhythm was infectious. Lord

Haywood twirled her with effortless grace, his eyes glimmering with amusement. Mariah's laughter escaped her despite herself, bright and unrestrained. The tension of the past weeks melted away as they spun across the floor, skirts and coats swirling like silk ribbons.

But her joy was short-lived.

As Lord Haywood extended his arm for another turn, another couple stumbled into their path. Mariah's slipper caught the hem of her gown, and she lurched forward. In an instant, Garrett's arm swept around her waist, pulling her firmly against his chest. Gasps rippled across the dance floor. Her cheeks flamed as she found herself pressed against him, her palms braced against the solid plane, of his chest. The faint scent of sandalwood, mingled with something warmer, wrapped around her senses.

"You're all right," he murmured, his voice low enough that only she could hear. But before she could respond, the shock and sudden motion made her head spin. Her breath quickened, the room tilted, and then darkness closed in.

When she came to, a cool, damp cloth pressed against her forehead. Her head throbbed faintly, and for a moment she could not remember where she was. Then she heard her father's voice and recognized the anxious tones of the dowager duchess.

"Mariah, my dear," Lady Haywood said soothingly, "you're safe. Just rest."

Mariah blinked her eyes open. She was lying on a fainting couch in one of the drawing rooms off the ballroom. The fire crackled softly nearby. Her father stood not far away, concern etched deep into his features. Beside her sat the dowager duchess, with Agnes and Nora hovering like worried mother hens. Before anyone could say more, the door opened and Lord Haywood entered the room. His usual composure appeared strained by worry.

"I've reassured our guests that Lady Mariah is recovering well," he told his mother, his gaze immediately finding Mariah. "Do you think we should send for a physician?"

The duchess shook her head as she turned toward her son.

"No, I believe rest is all she needs."

Lord Haywood stepped closer.

"How are you feeling, Lady Mariah?" he asked softly. "Shall I summon a doctor, just to be certain?"

Mariah met his gaze and instantly wished she had not. The warmth in his eyes undid her. She lowered her lashes quickly, willing her pulse to calm.

"Thank you, Your Grace," she murmured, "but I am quite all right. Please forgive me for causing a scene."

"Oh, you didn't cause a scene," Nora said at once, squeezing her hand affectionately. "This was no one's fault."

"Indeed not," agreed the dowager duchess, patting Mariah's cheek fondly. "It was merely the shock that overcame you. Fortunately, Garrett was near enough to catch you before you fell. He carried you here himself."

Mariah's breath caught. *He carried me?* Her cheeks warmed again, and she pressed her hand to her face.

"Thank you," she mumbled, unable to meet anyone's eyes. "For catching me... both times."

Lord Haywood smiled, the corners of his mouth lifting with unmistakable amusement.

"It was nothing, I assure you." Yet his gaze lingered on her, filled with quiet concern. As Mariah sat up slowly, everyone instinctively reached out, ready to steady her. The sight of four pairs of worried faces nearly made her laugh, though she masked it with a tender smile.

"Please don't fuss," she said gently. "I promise I'm not going to faint again."

"Still," Lady Haywood protested, "you ought to rest a little longer, dear."

"I will," Mariah assured her kindly. "Truly, I'm only shaken, not unwell."

Her father frowned. "Are you certain you don't need a physician, Mariah?"

She nodded, her tone firm.

"Quite certain. I only need a few minutes to compose myself. Please, go enjoy the evening. I'll rejoin you shortly."

The duchess rose, exchanged a knowing glance with her son, and led the Duke of Kent from the room. Lord Haywood followed, though he hesitated at the doorway long enough to give Mariah one last look, something soft and unspoken flickering across his face, before disappearing down the hall. Agnes and Nora remained behind.

"You gave us quite a fright," Agnes said, shaking her head.

"I truly didn't mean to," Mariah replied with a weak smile.

"Oh, hush," Nora said warmly, squeezing her friend's hand. "Mama was right, it was only shock."

They lingered until Mariah assured them, she felt steady again. Then, at her urging, they returned to the ballroom, promising to send for her if she did not appear soon. Once alone, Mariah let out a slow breath, pressing her fingers to her racing heart.

Twice in one evening, she thought, and both times in his arms. She could still feel the strength of Garrett Haywood's hold, the security of it, and it both comforted and unsettled her more than she dared to admit.

After washing her hands and dabbing her face with a cool cloth, Mariah left the washroom feeling refreshed and ready to rejoin the festivities. The faint strains of a waltz echoed down the corridor as she made her way back toward the ballroom. But before she reached the foyer, hushed voices caught her attention.

Curiosity pricked at her senses. She slowed her steps and, rounding a corner, spotted Susannah Brighton standing near the grand staircase with two of her usual companions. The three young women appeared to be waiting for someone, their heads bent close together as they whispered and exchanged sly glances.

A timid young maid stood just behind Susannah, balancing a silver tray laden with wine glasses. The poor girl's hands trembled beneath the weight. Moments later, an older gentleman emerged from the ballroom, Baron Brighton, unmistakably. The maid stepped forward to offer him a glass, bowing her head respectfully.

It happened in an instant. Susannah extended the tip of her satin slipper, barely a movement, but enough. The maid stumbled, gasped, and tripped over Susannah's foot, falling hard to the floor.

The tray clattered from her grasp, glasses shattering across the polished tiles. Crimson wine splashed everywhere, soaking the maid's apron, staining the baron's breeches, and, most catastrophically, spreading across the pale blue silk of Susannah's gown. The shriek that followed pierced the air.

"You stupid, clumsy girl!" Susannah cried, her voice trembling with outrage as she stared down at the spreading stain. "Look what you've done to my dress!"

The maid scrambled to her knees, tears streaming down her face.

"Please forgive me, Miss Brighton—My Lord," she pleaded. "I tripped."

Susannah's fury only intensified. She struck the girl sharply across the face.

"You begged to accompany us tonight, remember?" she snapped. "My father agreed, thinking it might help you find respectable employment. And this is how you repay our kindness? By humiliating us before half of Ashford?" Her voice dripped with venom. "Father, I insist Elizabeth be disciplined at once."

Mariah froze, her heart pounding. Elizabeth cowered at the baron's feet, trembling uncontrollably. Baron Brighton's jaw tightened.

"Stand up," he barked, seizing the girl roughly by the arm and yanking her upright. When she cried out in pain, he raised his hand as though to strike her. Before he could, Mariah stepped forward.

"That is enough!" Her voice rang through the foyer. Every head turned. "You have no right to treat this poor girl with such cruelty," she declared, her tone steady despite the outrage surging within her. Baron Brighton's gaze snapped toward her, his expression thunderous.

"This is none of your concern, Lady Mariah. I advise you to stay out of it."

"I do not care for your advice," she retorted, her chin lifting in defiance. "I will not stand by while you abuse someone weaker than yourself. Step away from her, now, or I will make a scene you will not soon forget."

He narrowed his eyes, clearly unaccustomed to being challenged, least of all by a young woman.

"Elizabeth," he said curtly, "fetch your coat and wait in the carriage. You will be disciplined at home."

Mariah's stomach twisted. "What do you mean by *disciplined*?"

The baron sneered. "Why, with the strap and cane, of course. It's the only language such girls understand."

Mariah gasped, horror flashing across her face.

"You cannot be serious. That is barbaric." She turned to the trembling maid. "Elizabeth, you will not return with them. You may come and work for my father and me. We will see to your protection."

"Lady Mariah—"

A deep, commanding voice cut through the tension.

"What is going on here?"

Everyone turned. The Ashford steward stood in the doorway, and beside him was the Duke of Ashford himself. Both men looked grim.

"Why is this young lady crying?" the duke asked, his tone deceptively calm. Susannah seized the moment at once.

"She ruined my dress, Your Grace!" she cried, gesturing dramatically toward the stains. "She will lose her employment because of her carelessness."

"That is not the reason she is crying," Mariah countered, stepping protectively in front of Elizabeth. "Miss Brighton struck her across the face, and the baron threatened her with the strap and cane."

Baron Brighton stiffened, his complexion darkening.

"How dare you spread such lies about me, Lady Mariah?" he thundered. "You despise my daughter and would say anything to damage our family's name, just as others did to my late father."

Mariah's eyes blazed. "I speak only the truth, and you know it. I saw your daughter trip her, deliberately, and I heard you threaten further punishment with my own ears."

The duke turned his attention to the frightened maid.

"Elizabeth," he said quietly but firmly, "does the baron or his family beat you? Have you been harmed in their service?"

The girl trembled. Her lips parted, but when she caught Susannah's furious glare and sensed her master looming over her, she merely shook her head. Susannah smiled sweetly.

"You see? She denies it."

Mariah's blood boiled. "Your Grace," she said urgently, turning to Lord Haywood, "please, look at her. She's terrified. I beg you to investigate. Miss Brighton tripped her deliberately to humiliate her. I saw it."

The baron stepped forward.

"Elizabeth is my servant, not His Grace's concern."

Lord Haywood's expression hardened, his voice suddenly sharp.

"On the contrary, Baron. When such conduct occurs under my roof, it becomes very much my concern." He turned to his steward. "Mr. Swan, see that this young woman is placed under the protection of my household until a full inquiry is completed. The Brighton family's treatment of servants will be investigated without delay." Then he faced the baron once more, his gaze icy.

"If Lady Mariah's account proves accurate, I will personally ensure your conduct is reported to the Crown and that your name is struck from the peerage register. Ashford will not harbor cruelty."

Silence descended, thick, suffocating. Baron Brighton's face turned a dangerous shade of red, but even he dared not challenge a duke. He bowed stiffly instead, fury barely contained.

"Come, Susannah," he hissed, gripping his daughter's arm as they turned and stalked toward the exit.

The rest of the evening passed in uneasy quiet. Mariah said little as she and her father returned to their carriage. He cast her several worried glances but wisely refrained from pressing her for explanations.

Only once she was safely in her chamber did the weight of the night's events truly settle upon her. Her heart ached for Elizabeth and burned with righteous anger at the Brightons' cruelty. At last, exhaustion claimed her, drawing her into a restless sleep.

The next morning dawned gray and cold. Snow fell thick and fast beyond the window, blanketing the countryside in white. Mariah rose early, packed a few extra clothes, and set out for the Haywood estate as planned. Nora had invited her to spend the day with them, and Mariah welcomed the thought of a quiet respite among friends.

After a brief visit to her grandparents' home, she rode on toward Conningbrook Hall. The journey was beautiful yet treacherous, the snowfall now so heavy that the distant hills disappeared beneath a silver haze.

By the time she reached the estate gates, the storm had settled in earnest. The wind howled across the frozen lake, flurries swirling about her cloak. Yet as she looked upon the charming and prestigious manor, she felt a strange, steady calm. Whatever awaited her inside, she would face it with courage.

"Mariah!" came the delighted call from the foyer, followed by a rush of footsteps. "Mariah, it is so good of you to come. I feared the snow might keep you away."

Mariah smiled as her friend threw her arms around her.

"It was quite the journey," she admitted, brushing the snow from her cloak. "But I could not bear to miss the chance to spend the day with you."

Before Nora could respond, the door to the study opened, and the Duke of Ashford stepped out. Firelight caught in his dark hair, and his expression softened the instant he saw Mariah.

"Lady Mariah," he greeted warmly, his deep voice carrying across the corridor. "It is wonderful to see you again."

Her heart fluttered wildly as she dropped into a curtsy.

"Your Grace."

Before she could rise fully, he took her hand and guided her upright with gentle pressure, his touch firm, yet careful. Their eyes met, and for one dizzying moment, the world beyond the walls, the storm, the howling wind, seemed to vanish.

"Thank you for braving the storm to come," he said softly, still holding her hand. Mariah managed a polite smile, even as her pulse refused to steady.

"It was no trouble at all."

Behind them, Nora's voice broke the spell with teasing amusement.

"Aren't you supposed to be in a meeting, Brother?"

Lord Haywood blinked, then chuckled and released Mariah's hand, though not before she caught the faintest trace of reluctance in his touch.

"Indeed, I am," he admitted, casting his sister a look of mock reproach. "But some interruptions are far too pleasant to ignore."

Mariah's cheeks burned crimson. Nora grinned knowingly as her brother inclined his head and disappeared back into his study. Once he was gone, Nora linked her arm through Mariah's.

"Come," she said lightly. "Let's take a turn through the gardens before the storm worsens. Once it sets in properly, we'll be trapped indoors for days."

Mariah nodded, grateful for both the distraction, and for the cold air that might cool the warmth lingering on her face.

The two women strolled in companionable silence, their boots crunching softly along the snow-dusted paths. The air smelled of pine and frost, and the gardens, blanketed in white, gleamed faintly beneath the pewter sky. When they reached the marble pavilion overlooking the frozen lake, Nora paused, drawing her cloak more tightly around her shoulders.

"Where is Agnes today?" Mariah asked, her voice calm, though her breath misted, in the cold air. Nora smiled wistfully.

"My sister will not be joining us much longer, I fear. She has formed quite the attachment to the Earl of Canterbury. He spends most of his time visiting his grandparents here in Ashford, and I dare say he will propose before Christmastide ends."

Mariah's heart lifted. "Oh, that is wonderful news. And what of you, Nora? I could not help but notice Lord O'Brien watching you rather closely at the ball. You seemed... quite taken with him."

Nora blushed, her eyes sparkling.

"I admit, I am rather fond of him. He is charming and kind, and he has already asked Garrett's permission to call this afternoon."

Mariah laughed softly. "Then I must offer my congratulations to you both. Your mother seemed equally fond of him."

"Oh yes, Mama has taken quite a liking to him," Nora said with a playful grin. "She also approves of the Earl of Canterbury. Lord O'Brien may only be a viscount, but that does not trouble us. I was a little afraid Garrett might disapprove, but he surprised me, he seems to like him very much."

Mariah sighed with mock despair.

"It seems I shall be left quite alone before the year is over," she teased. "You will all be married and gone, and I shall have no one to gossip with."

Nora laughed. "I doubt that very much. You might shock us all by marrying before Agnes or I are even engaged."

Mariah giggled, shaking her head.

"You flatter me, Nora. But who would I marry? I have no attachment to anyone."

Her friend's eyes twinkled with mischief.

"Have you not? I thought the attraction between you and my brother was quite obvious."

Mariah froze. Heat flared up her neck, and she looked away at once.

"I think you misunderstand," she murmured, her voice barely above a whisper. "It is not as it may have appeared."

Nora raised a brow. "Forgive me, but I cannot agree. From the very moment Garrett met you, he has scarcely looked at another woman."

Mariah swallowed hard. *That* was precisely the problem.

"Nora," she began carefully, "your brother made a promise, and I fear he is allowing his heart to be swayed when it should not."

But before she could say more, a deep voice sounded behind them.

"Lady Mariah, might I have a word with you?"

Her pulse leapt. Mariah turned to find the Duke of Ashford approaching through the snow, his dark cloak dusted in white. Nora grinned knowingly.

"I shall see what Mama's plans are for tea," she said brightly, giving Mariah's hand a squeeze before hurrying off, leaving the two of them quite alone.

Lord Haywood stopped before her, his breath clouding in the icy air.

"Thank you," he began quietly, "for standing up for Elizabeth last night. She finally spoke this morning. Everything you suspected was true."

Mariah's heart softened. "Oh, poor girl. Will she be safe now?"

"Yes," he assured her. "I have ordered that she remain here. The constables will investigate once the roads are clear enough for travel, and Baron Brighton will answer for his cruelty. He left this morning, in quite the rage."

Relief washed over her, and Mariah smiled.

"I am so grateful, Your Grace. She deserved to be believed."

He held her gaze, his expression unreadable yet unmistakably tender.

"You should know," he said softly, "I never doubted you."

The warmth in his eyes made her pulse stumble. She looked away quickly, twisting her gloved hands together.

"Was that what you wished to speak to me about, Your Grace?"

He hesitated, then shook his head.

"No," he said, stepping closer. "You already know what I wish to say."

"I'm afraid I do not," she replied, her voice wavering. "And I think I should return home. The snow—"

"Mariah." His hand closed around hers, gentle but firm. "Will you not look at me?"

"Your Grace..."

He lifted his free hand, his fingers brushing beneath her chin, tilting her face upward. The quiet intensity in his eyes stole her breath.

"Please," he murmured, "call me Garrett."

Her throat tightened. "That would not be proper. You are the Duke of Ashford. I cannot address you so familiarly."

"Not even," he asked quietly, "if I wish to become your husband?"

Her world stopped. "My—my husband?" she stammered, scarcely able to breathe. "We have barely met. You cannot mean—"

"I mean every word," he said, his voice low and fervent. "I have thought of little else since the night I met you. Tell me truly, will you deny that you feel this between us?"

Her lips parted, but no sound emerged. Longing and confusion warred within her, tightening her chest until it ached.

"I... cannot deny it," she whispered at last. "But I cannot marry you either."

"Why not?"

"Because," she said softly, tears pricking her eyes, "you made a promise to another woman, and you must honor it. You knew her long before you knew me. Whatever your heart feels now, you must set things right with her."

Garrett looked stricken. "What promise? To whom?"

"You know very well," she said, her voice breaking. "Please, Your Grace... keeping one's word is far more important than following one's heart." Before he could respond, she pulled her hand free, gathered her skirts, and fled through the snow.

"Mariah!" he called after her.

She did not turn. The wind had risen, carrying her name away on its icy breath as she ran toward the stables, her heart breaking with every step.

Mariah stopped only when she reached the stables, her breath coming fast and shallow. The icy wind stung her cheeks, and tears, hot and unbidden, blurred her vision. She pressed a trembling hand to her lips, willing herself not to cry.

Not yet, she told herself. *Not until I am far away from here.* She turned to one of the stable boys.

"Please saddle my horse," she said quickly, her voice shaking only slightly. "I must return home at once."

The boy nodded and hurried off. As she waited, muffled voices drifted from behind the barn. At first, she paid them little mind, but something in the low, urgent tones pricked at her senses. She hesitated, then moved a step closer. The voices sharpened, words taking shape. She recognized one of them instantly, the slick, oily drawl of Lord Dalton.

"What's the plan now, Uncle?" Dalton asked, his tone grim. "It seems everything has gone wrong since that wretched woman began interfering."

"We'll correct it soon enough," Baron Brighton replied coldly. "The Haywoods have meddled for the last time. We should have finished the job years ago, when we took care of the old duke."

Mariah's breath caught. Her gloved hand flew to her mouth.

The old duke... taken care of? Did that mean Lord Haywood's father had been murdered?

A third voice answered, low and unfamiliar, yet unmistakably deferential.

"Do you still have the poison left, Gordon?"

Mariah froze. Gordon, the Haywoods' own butler.

"Yes, My Lord," the servant replied smoothly. "I did not require much for the late duke, and there is still enough left for the rest of them."

"Good." Baron Brighton's voice was like ice. "Now, what are we to do about Lady Mariah? The girl caused quite a scene yesterday."

"I'll take care of her," Dalton growled. "That meddling little miss has crossed me twice now, first when she interfered with my maid, and again at the ball. She'll regret ever standing in my way."

12

The Bastard Heir

Mariah staggered back a step, her heart pounding so violently she feared it might betray her. She had to warn someone, *now*. She turned to flee but collided with a tall figure emerging from the stable. Strong hands caught her before she could fall.

"Lady Mariah?"

She looked up, relief surging through her, when she recognized Mr. Amistad Swan, the Haywoods' steward.

"Mr. Swan!" she gasped, clutching his arm. The concern in his eyes deepened as he took in her pallor and trembling form.

"My Lady, are you unwell?"

She shook her head quickly. "No, no, listen. You must go to His Grace. There's no time." She pulled him into a shadowed corner, her voice dropping to a desperate whisper. "The late duke, he was murdered. I heard them confess it just now. Baron Brighton and Lord Dalton. Gordon is helping them. They plan to poison the family."

The steward blanched. "Merciful heavens."

"Please," Mariah pleaded, her voice breaking. "They mean to harm the Haywoods *tonight*. Gordon still has poison. You must act quickly."

155

Amistad gave a sharp nod. "I will see to it at once. Stay here, My Lady, do not leave the stables until I return." He turned and sprinted toward the house.

Mariah had barely drawn a breath when a harsh voice cut through the swirling snow behind the barn.

"Lady Mariah!"

Her blood turned to ice. Lord Dalton stepped from the shadows. His face twisted with fury. Baron Brighton loomed just behind him. Mariah spun toward the manor and ran, calling for help, but she had taken only a few steps when Dalton lunged forward. His hand closed around her arm, yanking her back with brutal force.

"Let me go!" she cried, struggling wildly, but his grip was iron.

"Not this time, sweetheart," he hissed. His hand clamped over her mouth, smothering her scream as he dragged her across the frozen ground.

"Quickly," Baron Brighton barked. "Get her inside."

Dalton shoved her toward a waiting carriage, its dark shape barely visible through the driving snow. She kicked, twisted, even bit his hand, but he only cursed and forced her inside, slamming the door as soon as he had climbed in himself.

"Follow in a few hours," the baron ordered the men outside as he leapt in beside them. "Drive!"

The carriage lurched forward, wheels skidding as it plunged into the heart of the storm.

Back at the manor, Garrett Haywood had just returned to his study when movement beyond the window caught his eye, a carriage hurtling down the drive at reckless speed. For an instant, through the frosted glass, he glimpsed a flash of golden hair, a pale face. Mariah. He straightened, his pulse surging.

"What in the devil—?"

At that moment, Amistad burst into the room, his expression ashen. "Your Grace," he panted, "I believe Lady Mariah has been kidnapped."

Garrett's world tilted. "What?"

The steward wasted no time, relaying everything Mariah had told him. By the time he finished, Garrett's jaw had set into grim determination.

"Lock Gordon in the cellar," he ordered sharply. "See to it personally. Double the guards, my mother and sisters are not to be left alone. Send a rider to Lord Kensington at once and tell him exactly what has happened."

Amistad hesitated. "Your Grace, the storm—"

"I don't care about the storm," Garrett snapped. "If I cannot bring her home tonight, I will take her to the hunting cabin until it is safe."

Without another word, he turned and strode into the cold, the wind tearing at his cloak as he crossed the stable yard. A saddled horse stood waiting, Mariah's. He mounted in one fluid motion and spurred the animal forward, galloping straight into the blinding snow.

"Let me go!" Mariah shouted, her wrists chafing painfully against the ropes binding her hands. Dalton merely smirked, pinning her in place.

"You should have kept out of our affairs."

"Where are you taking me?" she demanded, turning a furious glare on the baron.

"To somewhere... quiet," Brighton replied coolly. "I have not yet decided whether to make you my nephew's wife or hold you for ransom. Either way, you, your family and the Haywoods will regret ever crossing me."

"You're both despicable!" she spat, struggling again. Dalton's grin only widened. He shoved her back onto the seat as the baron secured her ankles. When she tried to scream, Dalton gagged her roughly, silencing her with a curse.

The carriage rattled and swayed as it plunged deeper into the snow-choked countryside. Branches scraped against the windows, and the horses snorted and slipped on the frozen track, but the driver never slowed. Time blurred, minutes seemed to be stretching into hours, until the wheels jolted sharply, turning onto a narrow, rutted path. The trees closed in around them, their dark limbs clawing at the carriage as it forced its way through the forest. At last, the carriage ground to a halt.

Dalton flung open the door, leapt down, and dragged Mariah after him. She twisted in his grasp, fighting for purchase, but he merely hoisted her over his shoulder like a sack of grain. Through the veil of swirling snow, she glimpsed the outline of a small, crumbling cabin, half-buried beneath the drifts.

"Here we are," Dalton sneered. "Home sweet home."

The door slammed shut, behind them. Mariah's heart thudded painfully in her chest.

The stench inside the cabin struck Mariah at once, stale ale, mold, and decay. The air was thick and suffocating, heavy with dust and rot. The Earl of Wyndham carried her through the narrow entryway into what might once have been a bed chamber, now little more than a ruin. He dropped her unceremoniously onto a sagging, filthy mattress that creaked beneath her weight. Without a word, he drew a knife, sliced through the ropes binding her ankles, and yanked the gag from her mouth. The rough motion left her lips sore and raw.

"Try screaming," he sneered. "No one will hear you over the storm." With that, he turned and left the room. The heavy door slammed shut, followed by the rasp of a key turning in the lock.

Mariah sat motionless, trembling, her heart pounding so fiercely it echoed in her ears. There was no window, only darkness. Thick. Oppressive. Endless. A thin line of light seeped beneath the door, barely illuminating the grimy floorboards. Panic clawed at her throat, but she forced herself to breathe.

Think, Mariah. Think. She knew screaming would do no good. Anyone who might have heard her was miles away, and the storm outside howled so violently that even her own heartbeat seemed muffled by it. As her eyes adjusted to the gloom, she began to search the room. The furnishings were sparse, a cracked washstand, a crooked chair, a tattered rug. Then, atop a tall, dust-caked bookshelf, she spotted an old oil lamp. Her pulse quickened. If she could shatter it and find a sharp shard of glass, she might cut through the ropes binding her wrists.

But just as she lifted it, something else caught her attention, a faint glimmer from the far side of the room. A narrow wooden door stood slightly ajar. She moved toward it cautiously and eased it open. Beyond lay a small, empty closet, pitch-black save for a thin shaft of light filtering through a tiny hole in the wall.

Curiosity overcame fear. She crouched and pressed her eye to the opening.

To her astonishment, she could see directly into the adjoining room. Firelight flickered, casting long, warped shadows over two figures seated close together. The baron. And Lord Dalton. Their voices carried clearly through the hidden gap in the wall.

"So," Dalton drawled, "what now? What do you intend to do with Lady Mariah?"

Baron Brighton leaned back in his chair, swirling a glass of brandy.

"I have yet to decide," he said coldly. "But I am inclined to force her into marriage with you. If she refuses…" He shrugged. "Then we will have no choice but to dispose of her."

A cruel smile spread across Dalton's face.

"Oh, I doubt it will come to that. I rather like the idea of taming her."

"Do not underestimate her," Brighton snapped, his tone sharp. "If she is anything like her mother, she will not be easily subdued."

Dalton frowned. "Her mother? Everyone says she was a gentle, gracious lady."

"She was," Brighton replied darkly. "Until someone threatened those she loved. I learned firsthand just how fierce the late duchess could be."

Dalton tilted his head, confusion creasing his brow.

"You speak as though you knew her."

Brighton hesitated, only a fraction, then gave a humorless chuckle.

"Not exactly," he said. "But I am… connected to the family."

Dalton leaned forward. "Connected how?"

The baron exhaled slowly, his eyes gleaming with cold satisfaction, as though he had long been waiting to speak the truth.

"I am Lady Mariah's uncle."

Mariah's breath caught, a sharp, silent hitch in her chest. She clapped a hand over her mouth to smother the gasp that threatened to betray her, her heart hammering so violently she feared it might be heard through the thin walls.

Her uncle. The words struck like a thunderbolt, leaving her reeling. Her thoughts scattered, tumbling over one another in a frantic rush. Had her father known? Had he deliberately kept this man's existence hidden—*from her*, from everyone? And if he were truly her uncle, why did he bear the name Brighton and not Kensington? Unless... unless he was her mother's brother. The possibility sent a chill through her blood.

Her mother—gentle, loving, fiercely protective when it mattered. Had she known what her own brother was capable of? Had she feared him? Had she been silenced by him? Mariah's head swam with questions, with revelations that threatened to shatter everything she believed about her family and her past. Fear coiled tight in her chest, sharp and suffocating. But she forced it down.

Listen, she told herself fiercely. *You must listen.* Whatever truth lay buried in this man's confession, however terrible, it was her only weapon now.

Dalton stared at his uncle in disbelief.

"Her uncle? You mean... her mother's brother?"

Brighton shook his head. "No. I am her father's half-brother."

"What?" Dalton's eyes widened. "Does Lord Kensington know?"

"I doubt it," Brighton replied with a sneer. "Our father, Mariah's late grandfather, had an affair with a maid before he married the dowager duchess. When he learned she was with child, he made his decision. He could not risk scandal, nor could he marry beneath his station. So, he arranged for the woman to disappear quietly. He paid her well, and she vowed never to reveal the truth."

Dalton's brow furrowed. "I always believed Grandfather was your father."

"So did everyone else," Brighton said coolly. "After leaving the Kensington estate, my mother found employment with your grandfather. He, too, was childless at the time and, unwilling to abandon a woman in distress, took me in as his own. He told no one the truth." Brighton leaned forward, his voice dropping to a dangerous hiss.

"When my mother finally confessed that she had once served the Kensingtons, I began to suspect. But it was not until years later, after her death, that I found proof."

Dalton frowned. "Proof?"

Brighton nodded slowly. "When Gordon and I went hunting here, I discovered a hidden drawer in this very cabin. Inside were two journals, my mother's and that of her lover. In those pages, I learned the truth of my parentage."

Mariah stumbled backward, the revelation burning through her like ice. Her pulse thundered in her ears, but instinct quickly overrode shock. She could not afford to unravel, not now. She needed proof. Something tangible she could carry with her if she managed to escape this place alive.

The diaries. If Baron Brighton had uncovered the truth there, then those very books might hold everything, the lies, the murders, the poisonings. She had to find them. Moving with painstaking care, she slipped back into the filthy bedchamber. The floorboards creaked beneath her boots. Each faint sound magnified in the oppressive silence. She froze more than once, listening for footsteps, for voices, anything, but only the storm answered.

She searched again. The drawers, empty. The shelves, bare. Despair began to coil in her chest when her fingers brushed against an uneven patch of wood at the back of a wardrobe drawer. Her breath caught. Slowly, carefully, she pressed along the seam. The panel shifted, giving way just enough to reveal a narrow, hidden compartment. With trembling hands, she reached inside and touched something smooth and cold. Two small leather-bound books. Diaries.

Mariah's heart leapt into her throat. She drew them out, scarcely daring to breathe, then slipped them deep into the inner pockets of her cloak. Afterward, she replaced the loose panel and drawer with meticulous care, ensuring everything appeared exactly as before.

The urge to open the diaries, to devour their secrets, was nearly overwhelming. Her fingers itched, her mind raced. But she forced herself to stop. Knowledge could wait. Survival could not.

There might yet be more to learn. And if she hoped to live long enough to use what she had found, she needed every scrap of information she could gather.

Drawing a steadying breath, Mariah crept back into the narrow closet and pressed her eye once more to the tiny hole in the wall, listening, watching, and waiting.

"Does Susannah know any of this?" Lord Dalton asked. Baron Brighton exhaled sharply, rubbing his temple.

"No. Susannah isn't my daughter."

Dalton frowned. "She isn't?"

"My wife could not bear children," Brighton continued, his tone low and measured. "Much like your grandfather's first wife. But Gordon's wife gave him twin girls. A pity she was such an unhappy woman. Forced into marriage, miserable in her station, and in love with a young aristocrat far above her class. When she bore the twins, she ran off with her lover and left Gordon with the children." He sipped from his glass before continuing.

"Gordon begged me to help him find homes for the girls. So, we divided them. Susannah, I took and raised as my own. The other, Elizabeth, was placed with tenants of mine. She grew up among servants and, in time, became one herself."

Dalton shook his head in disbelief.

"Does the other girl know?"

"Oh yes," Brighton replied, his mouth twisting. "Elizabeth knows the truth. My wife discovered our secret years ago, discovered everything, in fact. When she learned that Gordon and I were behind the deaths of the late Duke of Ashford and the Duchess of Kensington, she threatened to expose us both.

Unfortunately, she had already confided in Elizabeth, her chambermaid at the time. So, I did what I had to do. I declared my wife insane and confined her to her rooms." His eyes burned with hatred.

"I forbade Elizabeth to speak a word of it, but she grew resentful, couldn't stomach serving in the house where her twin sister was treated like a lady while she scrubbed floors. I tried to keep her quiet through punishment, but I knew it wouldn't last. So, I planned to have her publicly disgraced or removed entirely. That little scene at the ball should have rid me of her, but Lady Mariah intervened and ruined everything." His fist came down hard on the arm of the chair.

Dalton leaned forward. "But why kill Lady Mariah's mother? What possible reason could you have for that?"

Brighton's eyes narrowed, and when he spoke, his voice was thick with venom.

"Because she stood in my way. She, and her husband, both. I should have been the Duke of Kent. I am the eldest son of Theodor James Kensington, the rightful heir to the title. But instead, I was cast aside, a bastard denied what was mine. When I learned that Cecelia was expecting, I swore she would never produce another heir to rob me further."

Mariah clutched her skirts, her body trembling.

Brighton continued, almost in a whisper of satisfaction.

"My wife was close to Cecelia. She brought her tea during her confinement to help with the bleeding. I laced that tea with poison. I had hoped she would drink it before the child was born, but fate delayed her hand. She drank it afterward, when the bleeding worsened. No one ever suspected. They believed she died in childbirth. And I made certain the child would soon follow."

Mariah's hand flew to her mouth to keep from crying out.

"I couldn't get near the infant," Brighton went on, "but when I learned that Gordon was courting the nursemaid, the foolish girl who doted on the duke himself, I saw my opportunity. I whispered poison into her heart instead. Encouraged her jealousy. Fed her pride. She took the child out of spite, desperate to wound the man she loved." He smiled, a cold, wicked thing.

"But before I could reach her to reclaim the child, the woman vanished. Took the baby with her. Clarice, I believe her name was. I never found either of them again."

Mariah backed away from the wall, her entire body trembling.

Clarice. The name struck like a lightning bolt. Her nurse. The woman who had raised her before Lord Winter took her in. Tears stung her eyes. Her mother had been murdered, her family deceived, her very existence reduced to a pawn in her uncle's twisted game. But she could not crumble, not now. She had to survive long enough to expose him. Her gaze fell on the oil lamp once more. A reckless, desperate plan began to form.

13

A Kiss by the Hearth

Mariah picked up the lamp, examining the slick glass in her hands. It was heavy and nearly full. Breaking it would be dangerous, but perhaps no more dangerous than staying where she was. She hesitated. If she simply tried to escape, they would catch her. She needed a distraction, something to lure them into her trap.

The idea struck like lightning. If she spilled the lamp oil across the floor, they would slip the moment they entered. It would buy her precious seconds. She unscrewed the metal top, careful not to spill too soon. Working quickly, she poured the oil in a wide pool across the floorboards in front of the door, leaving a narrow dry path for herself along the wall. Then she hurled the lamp against the far side of the room. The crash shattered the silence, glass exploding across the floor. At once, she began to scream.

"Help! Please, someone help me!" She pounded on the door, her voice high and frantic. Heavy footsteps thundered in response. The key turned. The door flew open, and both men charged in at once, slipping immediately on the slick oil. Their boots skidded out from under them, and they crashed hard to the ground, cursing violently.

Mariah darted past them, her skirts brushing the oil while her feet found the dry strip she had left. Before they could rise, she slammed the door shut and turned the key, locking them inside.

"Curse you, girl!" Brighton bellowed, pounding from the other side.

But Mariah was already running. She yanked the key from the lock and fled down the corridor, their furious shouts echoing behind her. Bursting into the open air, she slammed the front door shut and turned the key once more. The icy wind struck her face like knives, but it did not matter.

She was free.

Mariah had no idea where to go. The storm was ferocious now, wild, merciless, alive with wind and white fury. Snow fell in thick, blinding sheets, and the wind screamed through the trees like a living thing. It tore at her hair and skirts, making it nearly impossible to see, or breathe. Icy flakes bit her face, and her fingers were already numb with cold.

She could just make out the dark shapes of several fallen trees, their twisted limbs jutting from the snow like skeletons. The forest beyond looked impassable, yet staying was even more dangerous. The men would break free soon.

I can't stay here. Mariah took a step toward the edge of the porch, shielding her face from the wind, but before she could jump down, strong hands seized her from behind. A scream tore from her throat as she was slammed back against one of the porch beams. Pain exploded through her head as it struck the wood, and the world tilted. Stars burst before her eyes.

The carriage driver's furious face loomed over her.

"Thought you could run, did you?" he snarled, his foul breath hot against her cheek. She fought back blindly, kicking and twisting, but he was too strong. He dragged her toward the door, one arm crushing her ribs. Snow swirled around them, the roar of the storm mingling with her ragged breathing. Then, suddenly, a sharp thud.

The driver stiffened, his eyes going wide. A choked sound escaped him before he crumpled to the ground at her feet. Mariah staggered backward in shock, barely keeping her balance as his body fell heavily into the snow. She gasped when a tall figure emerged through the storm, dark cloak, gloved hands, snow-dusted hair.

"Mariah!"

It was Lord Haywood.

Garrett had not been far behind the carriage. Though the storm had grown brutal, he pressed on, hunched low against the wind, urging the horse forward through the blinding snow. He had lost sight of them for a time when the carriage turned into the forest, but the tracks remained visible, deep gouges cutting through the drifts.

He followed until he caught sight of the carriage stopped near an old hunting cabin. From a distance, he saw Lord Dalton carry Mariah inside, Baron Brighton close behind. The driver led the horses toward a nearby barn, struggling to calm them as the wind whipped around him.

Garrett waited until the man disappeared into the barn with the last horse. He was just about to move closer when a figure burst from the cabin. Mariah.

Garrett's heart seized. He drew his pistol and sprinted forward. The man caught her just as Garrett closed the distance, and a single, swift blow from the butt of the pistol sent the driver collapsing into the snow. Mariah stared up at him, wide-eyed, breathless, and trembling. Garrett grasped her shoulders, his voice low but urgent.

"You're safe now, Mariah," he said, his tone both fierce and tender. "Let me drag this scoundrel inside. Then we must leave."

She nodded weakly and hurried to unlock the door. Garrett hauled the unconscious man into the cabin, and the moment the door opened, angry shouts echoed from within, the baron and Dalton still trapped in the inner room. The door still held. Wasting no time, Garrett seized the knife from the driver's belt and cut the ropes binding Mariah's wrists. Her skin was red and raw where the rope had bitten into it. He took her hand firmly in his, his grip warm and steady.

"Come," he said, his voice brooking no argument. He locked the cabin door behind them, shrugged off his heavy coat, and wrapped it around her shivering shoulders. Then, with one smooth motion, he lifted her onto her horse before mounting behind her. Mariah clutched the reins, her hands trembling, but she was alive.

The ride was long and punishing. The storm thickened until the world seemed reduced to nothing but wind and white, the snow lashing at them without mercy. Mariah clung to the saddle, her body aching, her senses dulled by cold and exhaustion.

At last, Lord Haywood slowed the horse. Through the swirling snow, Mariah glimpsed the faint outline of a structure ahead, a small cabin nestled among the trees, its roof already bowed beneath the growing weight of snow.

"We'll shelter here," the young duke said, dismounting swiftly and helping her down. "Go inside. I'll take care of the horse."

Mariah nodded, her limbs trembling too violently for words. She staggered toward the door, pushed it open with numb hands, and stepped inside, grateful beyond measure for even the promise of warmth and safety.

The difference between this place and the one she had escaped could not have been more striking. The air was warmer, dry, and faintly scented with pine and smoke. A large hearth dominated the room, stacked neatly with kindling. Mariah hurried to it, adding several pieces of wood and striking a flame with shaking hands.

When the fire flared to life, light and warmth spilled across the cabin. She turned to look around properly and her breath caught. This was no mere hunter's shelter. It was a cottage, charming and beautifully kept. The furniture was polished, the rugs clean, and garlands of evergreen and ribbon hung across the mantel. Someone had even decorated it for Christmas: candles, pinecones, and a few bright berries arranged in a bowl on the table. It felt almost magical after the terror she had just endured.

She wondered if someone still lived here, and if they might return at any moment. The door opened again, and Lord Haywood stepped inside, snow clinging to his clothes and hair. He closed and bolted the door, shutting out the howling wind. The world beyond vanished into a blur of white.

Mariah stood near the hearth, watching him, unable to ignore how striking he looked in the firelight, broad-shouldered, hair tousled, eyes dark with concern. Heat rose to her cheeks, and she quickly turned away. Lord Haywood scanned the room and smiled faintly.

"You've already started a fire. Wonderful."

"I thought we might freeze otherwise," she said softly, managing a small smile of her own. "This is the most beautiful hunting cabin I've ever seen. Do you think it's right for us to take shelter here? Perhaps someone lives here."

That earned her a grin, warm, teasing, and entirely too charming.

"We don't have to worry about that," he said. "This is my cabin."

Her brows lifted in surprise.

He stepped closer. "This was my father's old hunting lodge. My mother adored it, so he made improvements over the years. It has been kept in good condition since."

"Oh," she breathed. "Then I suppose we're safe."

"For now," he replied, his gaze flicking toward the storm-blurred window. Mariah looked around again.

"Do you know where I might find lamps or candles?"

"Top shelf of the kitchen cupboard," he said, gesturing toward a side door. She fetched several candles, lit them from the fire, and placed them around the room until the space glowed softly with golden light.

"That should do," she murmured, more to herself than to him.

Garrett's gaze lingered on her, on the way her damp hair clung to her temples, on the exhaustion shadowing her eyes.

"You're soaked through," he said gently. "And shivering."

She turned toward him, startled, and his expression softened.

"There's a warm bath ready to be drawn in the adjoining room," he continued. "Would you like one?"

Mariah blinked. "A bath? In a hunting cabin?"

He chuckled, the sound low and rich.

"My father believed in comfort, especially after my mother began joining him here. You'll even find some of her and my sisters' gowns in the wardrobe."

He opened a door to reveal a cozy adjoining chamber.

"Through here."

Mariah hesitated only a moment before following him, her heart still racing, though not from fear this time, but from the unfamiliar warmth that seemed to linger in the space between them.

Garrett had only just opened the wardrobe when a sudden, deafening crash shattered the calm. The splintering of wood and breaking glass filled the air, followed by a fierce gust of freezing wind. Mariah screamed as a rain of sharp shards, exploded across the room. Before she could react, Garrett spun around and threw himself over her, shielding her with his body. The impact sent a rush of icy air through the cabin, the howl of the storm now echoing inside as snow and sleet scattered across the floor.

When the chaos finally stilled, Mariah clutched his arm, trembling. Her wide eyes darted toward the source of the noise and froze. A massive tree branch had crashed through the window, its jagged limbs stretching halfway into the room, glittering with ice. Outside, the rest of the tree swayed dangerously, groaning beneath the weight of snow.

Garrett straightened slowly, keeping one steadying hand on her shoulder.

"Well," he said with a rueful smile, his voice rough with adrenaline, "that is most unfortunate." He brushed a few shards of glass from his sleeve and met her gaze. "Thankfully, the other bedchamber has no windows. Let's gather what we can before this one turns into an icebox."

Mariah nodded, still shaken but resolute. Together they moved quickly. Garrett grabbing armfuls of blankets, pillows, and quilts while Mariah snatched several dresses and nightgowns from the wardrobe. The air had already grown biting cold, their breath visible in the lamplight.

"Careful," Garrett warned softly as she stepped over the broken glass. "We'll need to board this up before long."

"I'll be fine," she replied, her voice steadier now. "I've survived far worse tonight."

He gave her a look that was half admiration, half concern, but said nothing else.

They carried everything down the short hall into the second bedroom, a smaller, cozier room with wood-paneled walls and a narrow stove tucked into the corner. Garrett spread the blankets across the bed while Mariah stacked firewood nearby.

Her fingers shook as she struck the flint, but the moment the first spark caught, she exhaled in relief. The little stove crackled to life, filling the room with flickering light and the faint scent of smoke and pine resin.

When warmth began to seep back into her chilled limbs, she went to tend another fire, this time in the kitchen hearth. The cottage soon hummed softly with the comforting sounds of crackling wood and the occasional whistle of wind through the chimney.

Meanwhile, Garrett returned to the damaged room. He tore a thick woolen blanket from one of the trunks and nailed it across the doorway to block the draft. Satisfied that the worst of the cold would be contained, he turned his attention to more practical matters. Taking two iron buckets, he unlatched one of the smaller windows in the main room. The icy air stung his face, but no trees threatened this side of the cottage. He scooped the buckets full of fresh snow until they overflowed, then secured the window once more.

When he returned, Mariah was kneeling beside the fire, her hair escaping its pins and glowing like copper in the firelight. She looked up as he set the buckets down beside her.

"What is that for?" she asked, curious.

"For your bath," he replied with a faint smile. "The pump is frozen solid, so we'll have to melt snow."

Her lips parted slightly.

"You mean to heat all of this by hand?"

"I've done worse in harsher storms," he said lightly, rolling up his sleeves. "Besides, you've earned it after the day you've had."

Mariah felt her throat tighten. No man had ever spoken to her in such a gentle, practical way, not with pity, but with quiet care.

Together, they worked in companionable silence, taking turns adding snow to the iron kettle and pouring the warm water into the tub in the adjoining washroom. The rhythmic motions, the hiss of melting snow, the crackle of fire, the soft thud of their boots, created an almost peaceful cadence. At last, Garrett straightened, wiping his hands on a towel. Steam curled through the air, and the washroom glowed golden in the lamplight.

"That should do," he said softly. "There's plenty of warm water now."

Mariah met his gaze, gratitude shining in her eyes. The storm might still rage beyond the walls, but for the first time that day, she felt safe.

Warm from the bath and wrapped in a soft woolen blanket, Mariah sat before the great hearth. The fire crackled cheerfully, its orange glow casting shifting patterns across the walls. Dressed in one of Lady Haywood's old gowns and thick stockings, she felt almost human again, safe, warm, and comforted by the scent of pine and smoke that filled the little cottage. Outside, the storm still raged. Wind roared against the shutters, and snow hissed as it struck the windows, but within these walls there was peace. For the first time in what felt like days, she allowed herself to close her eyes and simply breathe.

The door to the washroom opened, and the faint sound of boots on the wooden floor made her look up. Lord Haywood stepped into the firelight, his hair still damp, from his bath, his shirt open at the collar, cravat missing, sleeves rolled to his forearms. Heat rose instantly to her cheeks. It struck her all at once that they were completely alone, and would likely remain so for hours, perhaps even days. The realization sent a jolt of panic through her chest.

Lord Haywood noticed her expression and softened his tone as he crossed to her.

"How are you feeling?"

"Much better," she replied, though her voice came out quieter than she intended.

He hesitated a moment before asking gently, "Would it be all right if I took a look at your head wound?"

"Your Grace—" she began, flustered, but he shook his head.

"Garrett," he corrected softly. He crouched before her, close enough that she could feel his warmth. His hand brushed lightly against her temple. Mariah's breath caught. His touch was gentle, almost reverent, yet it sent her pulse fluttering like a trapped bird. She closed her eyes. Afraid he would see the color burning on her cheeks.

"It's only a small bump," he said at last, his voice low. "You'll be all right."

When he sat beside her again, Mariah dared to exhale. She could still feel his nearness, his steady presence beside her, both soothing and unsettling.

"I noticed a staircase behind the bedchamber," she said at last, more to fill the silence than anything else. "Does the cottage have an upper floor?"

He smiled faintly. "It does. Four bedchambers in all. My father designed it so our family could stay comfortably, and the servants would have their privacy whenever they joined us. He was rather proud of that."

The wind howled again, rattling the roof beams, and both of them glanced upward.

"With weather like this," Garrett said, his brow furrowing, "we're better off staying down here. If another tree falls, it'll strike the upper floor first."

Mariah nodded, grateful for the fire and the thick walls shielding them from the storm. For a long moment, neither spoke.

"I am amazed," she began hesitantly, "that such a beautiful cottage exists. Your father must have loved it very much."

A wistful smile touched his lips.

"He did. This was his sanctuary. He came here when the burdens of his position grew too heavy. It gave him peace."

Mariah's eyes filled with tears. She swallowed hard.

"Did Amistad tell you... what Baron Brighton and the others have done?"

Garrett nodded gravely and brushed a tear from her cheek with the back of his hand.

"He told me enough. Father was in perfect health. Gordon must have poisoned his tea. He went to bed that night and never woke again."

"I'm so sorry," she whispered. "I can't imagine how hard that must be. I suppose your mother finds it difficult to return here now."

"She does," he admitted. "She hasn't been back since his death. Even Ashford is painful for her. That's why she lives mostly in London now."

Mariah hesitated before speaking again, her voice trembling.

"I learned more about Baron Brighton. He murdered my mother."

Garrett's eyes widened, but he did not interrupt. She told him everything she had overheard in that dreadful cabin, the poison, the lies, the manipulation, the claim that Brighton was her father's half-brother. As she spoke, his expression hardened from sorrow to quiet fury. When she finished, he drew a slow breath, visibly restraining his anger.

"It seems Brighton's hatred runs deeper than any of us knew. His envy is poison in itself."

Mariah nodded miserably. "He believes he deserves my father's title, that he's the rightful heir. And now... I fear he will go after my father next."

Silence fell again, broken only by the storm outside. Garrett's jaw tightened, but his voice was gentle when he finally spoke.

"We'll make certain he never harms anyone again."

Mariah looked at him, truly looked at him, and saw not only strength, but tenderness. Then his tone changed, soft but insistent.

"Tell me, Mariah... why did you run from me earlier?"

Her heart lurched. "I—" She hesitated, unable to meet his gaze.

"Have I misread the signs?" he asked quietly. "If I've done something wrong, tell me."

Her eyes filled again. "No, you haven't. I was just... confused. After hearing so many conflicting things about you, and then hearing Miss Esther crying, saying you'd promised her father on his deathbed to marry her—"

He blinked. "What? I never made such a promise, and her father is very much alive."

"What?" she repeated, startled. He gave a short, incredulous laugh.

"That sounds like Susannah's mischief. She's played similar tricks before, even during my sister's engagement."

"You mean... it was all a lie? They deceived me on purpose?"

He nodded firmly. "Undoubtedly. Susannah probably urged Esther to play along to make you doubt me. She's done worse to others."

Mariah's cheeks flushed with anger.

"How cruel, and childish! Why would they do such a thing?"

"They saw what I saw," he said quietly. "The spark between us. Susannah meant to separate us before we had the chance to truly know each other."

Mariah's breath caught. She rose abruptly, needing to move, to think, but before she could flee the moment, Garrett stood and caught her gently by the arm, drawing her close.

"Mariah," he said softly, "I've never met anyone like you. I didn't even know it was possible to fall in love so quickly, but you've taken hold of my heart, and I can't let go. I love you. I've loved you since the moment you tried to carry your own trunk into the house."

A shaky laugh escaped her lips as she met his smiling eyes.

"I wanted to give you time," he continued, "because I didn't want to frighten you. But each time I saw you, I loved you a little more, especially when you stood up for Elizabeth without hesitation. That courage removed every doubt." He lifted her chin gently, his gaze steady.

"So, I'll ask again, Mariah Kensington. Will you marry me? Will you let me love and protect you all the days of my life?"

Her heart thundered in her chest. She could scarcely breathe. The confusion that had plagued her vanished, replaced by clarity. She had once mistaken admiration for love, but this, this was real. Garrett was real. Still, a tremor of doubt lingered.

"What about my father? He's only just found me again. He may not wish me to marry so soon."

Garrett brushed a loose curl from her cheek, his fingers grazing her skin.

"Your father and mine once spoke of their hope that we might one day fall in love. He'll give us his blessing, I'm certain. And if he asks that we wait, then we shall. But I don't believe he'll oppose us."

Mariah hesitated again. "What if people learn we've been here alone, without a chaperone?"

He grinned, mischief flickering in his eyes.

"Then our engagement will simply have to be announced sooner than planned."

Her blush deepened to crimson.

"Susannah would turn it into a scandal," she murmured. "She'd relish the chance to ruin me."

His expression darkened. "What has she said to you?"

When Mariah repeated Susannah's slander from the shop, Garrett's jaw clenched.

"Vile creature," he muttered. "Her malice knows no bounds. But it doesn't matter. Those who truly know us will never doubt our honor."

"But people don't know me," she whispered. "I've lived my whole life in Norwich—"

He silenced her gently with his fingertips against her lips.

"Do not give her words power, Mariah. You are above her. Don't let these foolish geese define your worth."

Lowering his hand but holding her gaze, he asked again, softly, but with conviction: "Now that everything is clear, Mariah Kensington, will you consent to be my wife and make me the happiest man alive?"

Tears shimmered in her eyes as she smiled through them.

"Yes," she whispered. "Yes, I will marry you."

The joy that broke across his face was pure and unguarded. He drew her close, cupped her cheek, and kissed her. The kiss was gentle, sweet and fleeting, but it set her heart racing all the same. When they parted, they simply looked at one another, smiling as though the world outside had ceased to exist. Mariah was the first to find her voice.

"Was it your father who had this cottage decorated so beautifully?"

Garrett's smile returned, warm and fond.

"Yes. He loved coming here during Christmastime. My mother adored the holidays, so he had the staff come each December to make the place festive for her. Because of that, we began calling it Christmas Cottage."

"Oh, how wonderful," Mariah said softly. "I can see why she loved it. It's so cozy, and so very romantic." She hadn't meant the last word to slip out, but Garrett's amused grin told her he had heard it. He stepped closer, his voice low and tender.

"Then perhaps," he murmured, "it's fitting that this is where our story truly begins."

Mariah's breath caught as Garrett's gaze found hers and held fast. Golden firelight danced in his eyes, turning them molten amber, and the world seemed to shrink until there was nothing left but the two of them, the soft hiss of the fire, the thunder of her heartbeat, the steady rise and fall of his breath. She could not move, could hardly think. Something in his expression, so raw, so unguarded, stirred a trembling deep within her chest. Heat bloomed in her cheeks, spreading like wildfire until she felt it pulse through every vein, every trembling fingertip.

Then, without a word, Garrett reached for her. His fingers brushed her chin, light as a whisper, tilting her face upward. The touch alone sent a shiver coursing through her. For a heartbeat, he hesitated, his thumb tracing the edge of her jaw as though asking silent permission. When his lips finally met hers, the world fell away.

The kiss was deep and unhurried, warmth and longing entwined. The faint scent of pine and smoke clung to him, grounding her even as her knees threatened to give way. His hand slipped to the back of her neck, steadying her, holding her as though she were something precious and fragile, while her fingers instinctively grasped the front of his waistcoat to keep herself from falling. The fire crackled beside them, its glow painting them in gold and shadow. The wind roared beyond the walls, but its fury no longer reached them. For that single, stolen moment, there was no storm, no danger, no world outside, only the warmth of his mouth on hers, the steady thrum of his heart, and the breath they shared between them.

When at last he drew back, his forehead rested lightly against hers. They were both breathless, the silence between them trembling with everything they dared not speak. His thumb brushed her lower lip, and she felt his warmth again, his nearness, his scent, his heartbeat, drawing her back toward him like a tide she could no longer resist.

"Mariah," he murmured, her name a sigh against her skin. Her eyes fluttered open, meeting his gaze. The tenderness there nearly undid her. For one fleeting second, she wanted nothing more than to close the distance again, to forget propriety, forget fear, forget everything but him. But reason returned with sharp, painful clarity. Her heart raced far too quickly, her breath far too shallow. She pressed her fingertips to his lips before he could claim her mouth again.

"We are alone, Garrett," she whispered, her voice trembling. "Let's not play with fire." The plea in her tone softened the words, and he understood at once. He stepped back, his chest rising and falling as he fought to steady his breath. For a long moment, they stood facing one another, the air between them charged with unspoken feeling. At last, Garrett released a quiet sigh, half resignation, half admiration, and a faint smile touched his lips.

"You're right," he said, his voice rough but tender. "You always are." And though he turned away first, she could still feel his gaze lingering, warm as the firelight dancing across her skin. To break the charged silence, she glanced toward the hearth.

"The only thing missing here," she said softly, "is a Christmas tree."

Garrett's lips curved into a grin.

"We have one."

Mariah blinked. "What?"

"There's a tree in the shed behind the cottage, already cut and waiting to be brought inside."

Her face lit instantly, childlike delight replacing the earlier tension.

"Truly? But how would we ever reach it in this weather?"

"Come with me," he said, mischief glinting in his eyes as he took her hand before she could protest. His grip was firm, warm, reassuring. He led her past the kitchen and into a narrow pantry. At the far end stood a heavy wooden door. Garrett opened it wide.

14

Fateful Ambush

Mariah gasped. "That is incredible."

Beyond the doorway lay a small, covered passage connecting the cottage to a large shed filled with stacked firewood, barrels, and, leaning in one corner, a pine tree dusted with frost.

Garrett grinned. "My father was a clever man. He knew how unpredictable winters could be. He had this passage built so we could reach the firewood without stepping out into a blizzard. The well outside and the kitchen pump were his doing as well, he liked to be prepared for emergencies."

Mariah smiled, charmed by both the ingenuity and Garrett's boyish pride.

"Shall we put up the tree?" he asked, eyes twinkling.

"Absolutely!" she replied without hesitation, her voice bright with enthusiasm. Garrett laughed, a deep, hearty sound that made her smile widen, and stepped into the shed.

With a practiced motion, he lifted the small pine tree, carried it into the sitting room, and set it in a bucket half-filled with water to keep it fresh. He steadied it with care, adjusting its branches until it stood perfectly straight.

Mariah inhaled deeply. "I love the smell of pine," she murmured softly. Garrett turned toward her, amusement dancing in his eyes.

"Do we have anything to decorate it with?" she asked.

"In the cupboard over there," he replied, nodding toward a wooden cabinet near the fireplace.

Mariah hurried across the room, excitement bubbling in her chest. She opened the cupboard doors and let out a delighted laugh. Inside were boxes of old ornaments, garlands of dried berries, gilded walnuts, ribbons, and little hand-carved stars. She gathered everything she could carry and returned to his side.

Together, they set to work. They hung ribbons and berries, draped strands of golden thread, and placed delicate ornaments upon the boughs. Firelight shimmered across the decorations, painting the tree with a soft, golden glow. When they finished, Mariah stepped back and clasped her hands together.

"It's perfect," she said with a bright smile. "Now we only need to add the angel." She picked up the little carved figure from the table and turned toward him.

"Garrett, you're tall enough. You can reach it, can't you?"

Instead of taking the angel, he gave her a teasing grin, stepped closer, and, before she could protest, lifted her effortlessly by the waist. Mariah let out a startled gasp.

"Garrett! What are you doing? Put me down at once!"

"Not until you do the honors," he said, laughing as he steadied her easily in his arms. "Every lady should crown the tree at least once."

Despite herself, Mariah smiled. Balancing carefully, she reached up and placed the angel at the top.

"There," she breathed. "Now please, put me down before I faint."

Garrett lowered her slowly until her feet touched the floor. She released a long, shaky breath, her cheeks flushed.

"It looks beautiful," she said softly, gazing at the tree.

"Yes," Garrett replied, his voice low and warm. "She is."

Mariah turned, startled to find his eyes not on the tree, but on her. Heat flooded her cheeks again.

"I was referring to the Christmas tree," she said firmly, striving for composure.

"I know," he murmured, stepping behind her, his voice close to her ear. "But I can't help being distracted by something far more beautiful."

She swallowed, her heart fluttering wildly.

"You are quite distracting yourself, Your Grace," she managed, forcing a playful tone as she stepped away.

He chuckled softly. "Touché." Then, after a pause, "Are you hungry? Shall I fix us some supper?"

Mariah blinked, surprised. "You can cook?"

Garrett laughed aloud. "Is that so hard to believe?"

"Well, forgive me, but I doubt there are many dukes who can prepare a proper meal."

His grin widened. "My father rarely brought servants here unless my mother came along. He taught me how to fend for myself, how to build a fire, mend a boot, and make a decent stew. He said a man who can't look after his own needs doesn't deserve to call himself capable."

"I'm impressed, Your Grace," she said with genuine admiration, her eyes shining. He stepped closer, catching her hand in his.

"So was I when I came in and saw the fire already blazing. I daresay not many ladies could have managed that on their own."

Mariah smiled modestly. "Being an only child, I often begged our servants to teach me household tasks. I can even start a coal fire, though I much prefer wood. It's less messy, less complicated and doesn't take nearly as long."

His grin softened into something warmer.

"Every word you say makes you even more intriguing. Tell me, can you cook as well?"

"I'm better at baking," she admitted, eyes bright with amusement. "I can cook when I must, but if I have a choice, I'd rather bake."

"Then I must count myself fortunate indeed," he replied warmly. "If the pantry is well stocked, perhaps tomorrow you'll treat me to some of your pastries?"

"If we have the ingredients, I'd be delighted," she said with a laugh.

"We should have everything you need," Garrett replied. "The servants stocked the larder when they decorated the place. But for now, I am famished. I can't promise a gourmet meal, but it will be edible."

"That sounds wonderful, Your Grace—"

A sudden voice from behind them cut her off.

"That sounds wonderful indeed. I am very hungry."

Both turned around in shock.

"Miss Brighton," Garrett said, his tone turning glacial as his expression hardened in an instant. "What are you doing in my hunting cabin?"

Susannah Brighton stood framed in the doorway, snow clinging to the dark folds of her cloak, her breath faintly visible in the cold air. Her eyes, sharp with venom, swept the room before settling on Mariah.

"I shouldn't be surprised to find you here, Lady Mariah," she said with icy disdain. "I always suspected you were quite familiar with His Grace after your extended stay in his house in London."

Garrett's fury flared at once, his jaw tightened, his gaze darkened, but before he could speak, Mariah stepped forward, placing herself squarely between them.

"Miss Brighton," she said, her voice steady, resonant with quiet authority, "I have told you before that I will not tolerate your obscene insinuations." She did not waver. "I am here because I was kidnapped by the Earl of Wyndham and Baron Brighton after overhearing them confess to murder, the murder of the late Duke of Ashford, among others. Lord Haywood rescued me, and we sought shelter here to survive the storm." Her gaze sharpened. "Now tell me, what, pray, is *your* excuse for being here?"

The color drained from Susannah's face. Her lips parted, but no words followed.

"Nothing to say?" Mariah continued, her tone keen as steel. "Then allow me to venture a guess. It is common knowledge that the Duke of Ashford keeps this cabin prepared for winter visits. Baron Brighton likely sent you here to hide, so that when he and his accomplices arrived, they might conveniently 'discover' you in a compromising situation with the duke." Mariah held her gaze, unflinching.

"A forced proposal would follow, sparing your family scandal while binding His Grace to you. Is that not so?"

Color flooded Susannah's face. "I—I don't know what you mean," she stammered, though her voice trembled. Mariah sighed.

"Listen to me. I have no desire to argue, but you deserve to know the truth. There are things Baron Brighton has kept from you, terrible things."

Before Susannah could interrupt, Mariah recounted everything she had overheard in the cabin, the confessions, the murders, the secrets of blood and betrayal. Susannah's face twisted with disbelief, fury, and confusion. She opened her mouth several times, but Mariah pressed on, unwilling to let her speak until she had finished.

At last, Mariah handed her the two worn diaries.

"These belonged to my grandfather and your grandmother," she said quietly. "I have not read them yet, but I believe they contain the truth, about Baron Brighton, about his parentage, perhaps even about you and your sister. Whatever that truth may be, it is yours to discover."

Susannah stared down at the diaries, her hands trembling. Her face was pale, her lips quivering, not only with rage, but with something deeper. Mariah watched closely and saw it, the flicker of doubt, of dawning realization. For the first time, Susannah Brighton, so proud, so venomous, looked uncertain. And perhaps, just perhaps, she knew that Mariah was telling the truth.

Susannah sank into a nearby armchair, her hands trembling as she opened the first page. Garrett excused himself and went into the pantry, intent on filling a basket with firewood. The air in the cottage was quiet but tense, the only sounds were the soft rustle of turning pages and the steady howl of the wind outside.

Mariah watched Susannah for a moment. The older woman's expression shifted from disbelief to confusion, then to something perilously close to fear as she read. Mariah turned toward the pantry, intending to help Garrett with the firewood. She had not taken even two steps when a strong arm snaked around her from behind, and a rough hand clamped tightly over her mouth. Her muffled cry was swallowed by the roar of the storm.

Before she could fight back, the front door burst open. Bitter wind and snow swept inside as Baron Brighton strode in, flanked by two burly footmen. His cold, calculating gaze swept the room before fixing on the pantry door. From within came the faint creak of wood.

"Search in there," the baron ordered. One of the men stepped forward, glanced into the small space, drew a pistol from his coat, and fired into the pantry without hesitation. Mariah screamed, but only a strangled sound escaped beneath the Earl of Wyndham's hand. The shot thundered through the cabin. Glass shattered, wood splintered, and then... silence.

Susannah dropped the diaries with a cry and rushed forward, shoving the footman aside.

"No!" she screamed, horror tearing from her throat as she stumbled into the pantry and fell to her knees beside the fallen figure.

"You didn't expect that, did you, Mariah?" Lord Dalton hissed against her ear. His breath reeked of whiskey as he dragged her closer, forcing her to look.

Through the open doorway, she saw Susannah kneeling on the pantry floor, sobbing uncontrollably beside Garrett's still body. Blood stained the wood beneath him. Mariah's heart stopped. Her knees buckled, and she would have collapsed had the earl not been gripping her so tightly.

"Why did you do that?" Susannah screamed at the baron, her voice breaking. "Why did you kill him?"

Baron Brighton's expression was cold, utterly devoid of remorse.

"He deserved it," he said simply. Before he could say another word, the front door burst open again. The cottage filled with shouts and chaos as Lord Kensington's steward, Mr. Wellington, stormed in alongside Garrett's steward, Amistad Swan, several footmen, and two constables.

Lord Dalton cursed and tried to retreat toward the back room, the one with the broken window, but before he could reach it, the butt of a rifle came down hard against his skull. He collapsed instantly, blood trickling from his temple.

Amistad seized Mariah, tearing her free and guiding her toward safety.

"This way, My Lady," he said firmly, his tone both commanding and protective. He ushered her into the adjoining room and shut the door behind her. Shouts, scuffling, and more gunshots rang out, but Mariah barely heard them. The world blurred through a haze of grief and disbelief.

Garrett—her Garrett—was gone. Her heart splintered inside her chest. She pressed a trembling hand to her mouth, fighting to breathe as the walls seemed to close in around her. When another gunshot cracked through the air, Mariah bolted for the window. She climbed over the fallen tree branch blocking it and stumbled out into the snow, her tears swallowed by the storm.

Inside, chaos still reigned. Baron Brighton stood in the center of the room, glaring at the men surrounding him. His expression was unreadable, but hatred burned in his eyes like coals. Two constables advanced, pistols drawn.

"You are under arrest, My Lord," one of them announced. The baron sneered and lunged. He was quickly overpowered, his arms twisted behind his back and bound with rope. Susannah stood motionless, staring at the man she had called her father all her life.

"Why did you have to kill him?" she whispered, her voice raw from crying. "He didn't even have a chance to defend himself."

"He deserved nothing but death," the baron snarled. "His family destroyed mine. And I don't understand why you're making such a fuss now. You wanted to hurt that Kensington girl for taking him from you."

Susannah's head snapped up, fury blazing in her eyes.

"I never wanted anyone to die!" she shouted. "Is that why you sent me here? You planned this all along?"

Brighton's silence told her everything. Her face drained of color as the truth dawned.

"Everything Lady Mariah told me was true," she whispered, stumbling back until she found a chair and collapsed into it. "You aren't my father. You're my half-uncle. Elizabeth is my sister. You murdered your own father, the late Duke of Ashford, the Duchess of Kensington, and you lied about Mama losing her mind."

The baron's eyes narrowed dangerously.

"Careful what you say."

Susannah rose again, trembling but defiant.

"Mama wasn't insane, was she?" Her voice shook. "You locked her away because she knew the truth. You beat her. You terrified her. And you made me believe it was for her own good."

He scoffed, his mouth curling into a cruel smile.

"I can't believe I ever trusted you," Susannah said bitterly. "You used me. You made me hurt people who never wronged us. You made me hate the Haywoods, all because of your jealousy and spite."

Brighton's eyes darkened. "It wasn't difficult to persuade you," he said coldly. "You were eager enough to obey. Every time I whispered poison into your ear, you drank it willingly. Why do you think I encouraged you to pursue the Marquess of Watford? Because the eldest Haywood girl loved him. It pleased me to watch you make her miserable, even if it didn't last."

Susannah's hand flew to her mouth, horror flooding her features.

"You used me," she whispered. "You made me punish Elizabeth, didn't you?"

"Yes," he replied without hesitation. "Your mother told her the truth, that you were sisters, and the foolish girl couldn't keep it to herself. I beat her into silence, but she was too much like her mother, too brave for her own good. I knew she would betray me eventually."

Susannah's voice broke. "You were going to kill her?"

The baron laughed. "Kill her? I should have, years ago. Gordon wanted her to be gone as well. He hated both of you, resented you for being born. He helped me murder the late Duke of Kensington to avenge our mother. She died bitter and ruined because of that man's lust and lies." He drew a breath, his tone turning venomous.

"That is why I wanted Elizabeth removed. With her gone, there would have been no one left to reveal what truly happened. But that pathetic, meddlesome Kensington girl interfered, just as her bloody mother once did."

Amistad stepped forward, his face carved from stone.

"Watch your tongue, Brighton," he growled, seizing the baron by the collar. "You are speaking of the Marchioness and the late

Duchess of Kent. Show some respect, or I will make certain you regret it."

Brighton sneered, but the cold fury in Amistad's eyes silenced him. The constables tightened their grip and dragged the baron toward the back room, locking him inside beside the unconscious Lord Dalton. When the door slammed shut, the room fell eerily quiet.

Susannah stood where she was, staring at the door that had just closed behind the man she had once believed was her father. For a long while, she did not move. When she finally spoke, her voice trembled with disbelief and grief.

"How could I have been so blind?" she whispered. "He was a monster, and I never saw it. He turned me into a monster too."

Amistad turned toward her, his tone gentler now.

"You were deceived, Miss Brighton," he said quietly. "He fooled many people. But the truth has a way of coming out... even through the storm."

Susannah nodded faintly, but her gaze drifted toward the pantry, toward where Garrett had fallen. Her hand rose to her mouth once more as silent tears streamed down her face. Outside, the wind howled against the cabin walls, carrying away the last echoes of gunfire, of lies, and of all the illusions that had bound them to the past.

When Mariah stood outside the window she had just climbed through, the snow was still falling thickly, though the blizzard had softened to a restless whisper. The world felt muted, too quiet, too still. Her heart ached so fiercely she wanted to scream, to let the grief tear its way out of her chest. But she bit it back, glancing around the snow-covered yard in desperate search for somewhere, anywhere, she could hide and finally break apart.

Her gaze fell upon the barn, half-buried beneath a drift of snow. Wrapping her arms around herself, she trudged through the white expanse, each step a battle against the cold and the heaviness in her limbs. When she reached the small building, she pulled the door open and slipped inside, shutting the storm out behind her.

The air smelled of hay and horses and faint wood smoke. Her mare nickered softly, but several unfamiliar horses filled the space now, clearly belonging to the men who had come to the cottage. Avoiding their restless movements, Mariah climbed the narrow ladder to the hayloft and collapsed into the straw. Only then did she break.

The sobs came hard and violent, shaking her from head to toe. She buried her face in her hands, gasping for air between each wrenching breath. Her heart felt splintered beyond repair. How could she have known such joy, such dizzying, all-consuming happiness, only to have it ripped away in the blink of an eye? Why him? Why Garrett?

Her tears soaked into the hay as the wind howled outside, the storm swelling once more in furious waves. But she no longer cared. Let it rage. The pain inside her was far greater than anything nature could unleash.

15

Rose Petals on Snow

Back inside the cottage, the confrontation reached its breaking point.

"You are a vile, wretched excuse for a human being, Brighton," James Kensington thundered as he strode into the chamber, his coat still flecked with snow. More footmen followed at his heels, armed and grim. "What you have done to our families makes even the devil look righteous."

The baron scoffed, his hands bound tightly before him.

"I do not care what you think of me," he spat. "I should have been the duke, not you. I was the firstborn, the rightful heir! My only crime was that my mother was a servant."

James stared at him as though he had lost his senses.

"What in the devil's name are you raving about?"

Before Brighton could answer, Susannah stepped forward, clutching the diaries to her chest. She sank into a trembling curtsy.

"Forgive me, Your Grace," she began softly, "but Lady Mariah uncovered the truth. The baron is not who we believed him to be. He is your father's illegitimate son."

James froze. "What?"

In halting words, Susannah explained everything she had learned, her voice breaking as she recounted the baron's confession, the deceit, the murders. When she finished, James sank heavily into a chair, his face pale, his expression one of stunned disbelief. For several minutes he said nothing, the weight of betrayal pressing the air from the room. Finally, he nodded to his steward.

"Close the door."

When it was done, he looked up again.

"Do you know where my daughter is?" he asked at last, his tone quiet but commanding. Before Mr. Wellington could respond, Amistad cleared his throat.

"I made certain she was out of harm's way when we entered. I left her in the room behind us."

A footman stepped forward hesitantly.

"She isn't there anymore, Your Grace. I saw her running toward the barn before the storm worsened again."

James exhaled, his expression softening with both worry and resolve.

"Thank you."

In the hayloft, Mariah sat before the tiny window, watching the storm consume the world outside. Snowflakes whirled through the dim light like ghosts, and tears continued to spill down her cheeks. The past weeks had tested her beyond endurance, secrets, betrayals, danger, but nothing, nothing had cut as deeply as losing the man she loved. This place, once warm and magical, would haunt her forever now. Even Christmas would never again feel joyful. It would always remind her of this night, of love found and lost in the same breath. She heard the barn door creak open and faint footsteps on the ladder. She didn't turn.

"Not now, Papa," she said hoarsely, her voice barely more than a whisper. "Please. I need to be alone."

The footsteps continued. Hay rustled behind her. She closed her eyes, bracing herself, until strong, familiar arms slipped around her waist and gently drew her backward. The warmth of that touch stole her breath. A gentle hand lifted her chin. Her eyes flew open, and the world stopped spinning.

"Garrett," she breathed, her voice breaking. He smiled faintly, his face pale but alive, his brown eyes soft and shining in the dim light. Before she could speak, she flung her arms around his neck, sobbing anew as he held her close, his hand stroking her hair.

"I'm so sorry you had to see all of that," he murmured against her temple. "I never meant for you to suffer. I never imagined they would come here during the storm."

She pulled back just enough to look at him, her tears shimmering.

"But how?" she whispered. "I saw you fall. I saw the blood. I thought you were gone."

He gave a small, reassuring smile.

"I'm very much alive, my love. It was all a ruse."

Her brow furrowed in disbelief, and he continued softly.

"Amistad and I prepared for this sort of danger after my father's death. We never trusted Brighton or his men, so we planned for every possibility. One of my footmen, loyal to us, fired the shot. It missed me, by mere inches. I dropped to the floor to make them believe I'd been struck. It was the only way to stop them from aiming again before our men arrived."

Mariah's hand flew to her mouth, her eyes wide.

"You pretended to be dead? But there was blood—"

Garrett nodded, his expression tender but resolute.

"It wasn't real. Amistad keeps small jars of stage blood at each of our properties, an odd precaution, I admit, but one that has proven useful more than once. After I brought you here, I suspected Brighton's men might follow, so I slipped one of the jars into my waistcoat pocket before stepping out to fetch firewood. When the moment came, I used it." He exhaled slowly, his gaze holding hers.

"It bought us precious time. Amistad and the constables were able to act without endangering you, or me." Then, softer still, he added, "It nearly broke me, seeing the look on your face and knowing you thought I was gone. But I had no other choice, Mariah. I had to protect everyone... especially you."

Her tears flowed anew, but this time from pure relief. He cupped her face between his hands, his thumbs brushing them away.

"You are not dreaming," he whispered. "I am here, alive, and I am holding the woman I love."

She smiled through her tears, a shaky, radiant thing, and pressed her forehead to his chest.

"I thought I'd lost you," she murmured.

"Never," he said firmly. "Nothing in this world will keep me from marrying you."

She wrapped her arms tightly around him, holding on as though she would never let go. For a long while they stayed that way, two hearts beating together in the quiet sanctuary of the hayloft while the storm raged outside.

At last, Garrett stood, still holding her hand.

"Come, my darling. The storm is worsening again. It's warmer in the cottage." He climbed down the ladder first, then helped her follow, steadying her as she reached the ground. She looked up at him, alive, whole, and impossibly dear, and for a moment could only stare, still struggling to believe he was real.

"Oh," he said suddenly, turning to her with that familiar teasing glint in his eyes. "I almost forgot something."

Before she could ask what, he swept her off balance, dipped her backward, and captured her lips in a fierce, breath-stealing kiss. Mariah gasped, her hands clutching his shoulders as the world melted away. The kiss held everything, his relief, her joy, their love that had defied death itself. When he finally drew back, his grin was warm enough to melt the snow outside. She could only gaze at him, dazed, her pulse racing. He steadied her gently, brushing a lock of hair from her cheek.

Then a deafening crack split the air.

They turned toward the door just in time to see a massive tree crash to the ground, its heavy branches blocking the entrance completely. Garrett's arm came around her in instinctive protection as the wind howled anew, furious and relentless. They were trapped again. Together.

The footmen wasted no time restoring order to the cottage. Under the stewards' direction, they carried the two criminals into the cramped servant's room behind the kitchen and secured them there. To make the remaining space livable, others turned their attention to the wrecked chamber where the window had been shattered by the falling tree.

Working quickly in the frigid air, several men heaved the heavy branches out through the broken frame and cleared away the worst of the debris. Once the last shards of glass were swept aside, they set about creating a temporary barrier against the cold. A thick woolen blanket was once again nailed across the opening, and the sturdy wardrobe was pushed in front of it for extra protection. Though makeshift, it did the job.

Soon after, one of the footmen lit a fire in the small cast-iron stove, its faint orange glow gradually chasing away the chill. The men exchanged weary glances but said nothing, they had all seen more than enough chaos for one night.

In the sitting room, James Kensington paced before the hearth, his expression was drawn and tense. The fire burned low, but he scarcely noticed. His thoughts were elsewhere, on his daughter, on Garrett, on the storm that refused to relent.

"Why hasn't he returned?" he muttered, more to himself than anyone else. "They should have been back by now."

Mr. Wellington stepped closer, his calm composure barely concealing his own concern.

"Your Grace, please, Lord Haywood knows these woods. He will keep Lady Mariah safe."

James turned sharply toward him.

"Safe, yes, but her reputation..." He trailed off, pressing a hand to his forehead. "If anyone learns she spent the night alone with him—"

Before he could finish, Amistad Swan entered, brushing snow from his shoulders.

"Your Grace," he said carefully, "two of our men have just returned from checking the grounds. A large tree has fallen directly in front of the barn, blocking the doors entirely. The snow is too deep to clear, and the storm has not yet eased enough to make a rescue safe."

James exhaled heavily, his shoulders sagging.

"Trapped," he murmured, staring into the fire.

Amistad's voice softened. "The barn is sturdy, Your Grace, and stocked with hay and blankets. They will have warmth enough to last the night. We can only wait for the wind to calm."

Reluctantly, James nodded. "Very well. But the moment this storm passes, we go for them."

When Mariah awoke, it took her a moment to remember where she was. The faint rays of morning sunlight filtered through the hayloft's small window, turning the world around her soft gold. The blizzard had passed. The air was still and heavy with the scent of pine and fresh snow. Garrett was still asleep beside her, one arm resting protectively across her waist. His coat and two horse blankets covered them both, the warmth of his body a quiet comfort through the long, frozen night.

For a moment, she simply watched him, his hair tousled, lashes dark against his cheek, the faint curve of a smile lingering even in sleep. Gratitude and wonder welled within her. He was alive. After everything, they had survived. Carefully, she slipped from beneath the blankets and crossed to the small window. The forest beyond, glittered in the morning light, a breathtaking landscape of white and silver. Icicles sparkled along the eaves, and every tree seemed dipped in frost. The world looked reborn, calm, clean, untouched.

Behind her, she heard Garrett stir. When she turned, he was already watching her, warm brown eyes meeting hers with the same steady tenderness that always made her breath catch.

"Good morning," he said, his voice low and husky with sleep. She smiled faintly.

"Good morning. The storm has passed. It's beautiful outside."

He rose, stretching carefully so as not to strike his head on the low rafters. Even so, he had to stoop beneath them.

"We need to get back to the cottage," he said, glancing toward the window. "Your father must be beside himself with worry."

Mariah nodded, brushing a stray lock of hair from her face.

"I imagine he's pacing holes into the floor by now."

Garrett stepped beside her to look out. Snow lay deep, nearly to the windowsill, but gleamed softly beneath the morning sun.

"If we climb out here, we should land safely," he said, studying the drift below. "It's deep enough to cushion the fall."

She gave him a dubious look. "And if it's not?"

He grinned, that familiar playful spark in his eyes.

"Then I'll catch you, of course. I've no intention of letting you fall."

Warmth rose to her cheeks. "You seem quite certain of yourself, Your Grace."

He leaned closer, his breath brushing her ear.

"When it comes to you, Mariah Kensington, I'm certain of everything."

Her pulse quickened, and for a brief, breathless moment, she almost forgot the world beyond that hayloft. But Garrett turned back to the window and pushed it open. A rush of cold air swept in, biting and clean. He climbed onto the ledge and glanced back at her with a reassuring smile.

"Stay close behind me."

Mariah took one last look at the golden light spilling across the hay and the warmth they were leaving behind. Then she drew a deep breath and nodded.

"All right. Let's go."

Garrett dropped down first, disappearing into the drift below with a soft thud. A moment later, his voice rose from beneath the window, calm, steady, familiar.

"All right, my love. Jump. I'm here."

And without hesitation, Mariah leapt into his waiting arms.

They burst into the cottage just as Lord Kensington and his footmen were preparing to brave the cold in search of them. The door flew open, letting in a rush of icy wind and sunlight reflected off the snow.

"Mariah!" Her father crossed the room in an instant, pulling her into his arms. She clung to him, tears spilling freely as his hands pressed against her back, reassuring himself that she was truly safe. For a long moment, neither of them spoke. The sheer relief in his embrace said everything words could not.

When at last he released her, Susannah hesitated a few steps away before approaching. Her posture was timid, her expression uncertain.

"Lady Mariah," she began softly, "I owe you an apology, one I fear is long overdue." Her voice trembled, but there was a sincerity in her eyes Mariah had never seen before. "You were right. About everything. The diaries confirmed it. The baron lied about who he was... and about who we all were. He's responsible for the deaths of more than one innocent soul."

Mariah's brow furrowed.

"So, it's true, then? The baron murdered my grandfather, my mother, and the late Duke of Ashford, and deceived his own family?"

Susannah nodded, shame flickering across her face. Mariah turned toward her father, confusion and disbelief mingling in her expression.

"Papa... did you know your father had an illegitimate child before he married Grandmama?"

Lord Kensington's face paled. He shook his head gravely.

"No. I had no idea I was related to the baron in any way. I can scarcely believe it myself." His voice dropped, heavy with regret. "And I am almost certain my mother never knew either. My father must have carried that secret to his grave."

"Should we tell her?" Mariah asked quietly. James Kensington sighed and looked toward the window, where the snow still glistened beyond the glass.

"No, my dear. What good would it do? It would only wound her. Brighton will face justice, perhaps even the hangman's noose. There is no reason to reopen old wounds over something my father did long before he married her."

The others in the room murmured their agreement, even Susannah lowering her gaze in acknowledgment. After a moment, Mariah turned to Garrett's steward.

"Mr. Swan, may I ask... why wasn't Baron Brighton ever arrested before now? Elizabeth came to you. She tried to warn you, didn't she?"

Amistad Swan straightened, his calm dignity unshaken.

"She did, My Lady. But there was no proof, no evidence that would hold, in court. Elizabeth had spoken to the late Duke of Ashford not long before his death, but at that time she revealed only what the elder Lord Brighton had done, not his son. She feared implicating herself."

"Why didn't she come forward with the full truth?" Mariah pressed. Susannah stepped closer, her face somber.

"Because she was terrified," she said quietly. "Baron Brighton ruled his household through fear. He threatened anyone who dared to speak against him. I heard him warn Elizabeth more than once that if she ever betrayed him, he would take his anger out on the baroness or kill her outright." Her voice faltered. "I never thought he truly meant it. I believed they were only words meant to frighten. But after everything that has come to light... I see now that he was capable of anything."

Silence settled over the room, heavy and contemplative. Then, Garrett stepped forward. His hand was steady as he turned to Lord Kensington.

"Your Grace," he said, his voice clear and sincere, "I have loved your daughter from the moment I met her. She is brave, compassionate, and has a heart unlike any I have ever known. With your blessing, I wish to make her my wife."

James Kensington's stern composure softened into a warm smile. He clasped Garrett's hand, then turned to embrace his daughter once more.

"You have my full blessing, my boy," he said with genuine joy. "I could not have wished for a better man for my Mariah."

Tears shimmered in Mariah's eyes as Garrett pressed a tender kiss to her hand.

The following two weeks passed in a blur of joyous preparations for the wedding of Lady Mariah Kensington and Lord Garrett Haywood, Duke of Ashford. Invitations were sent far and wide, to Lord Winter and his household, to Mariah's childhood friends, and even to Lord Winter's loyal steward and housekeeper, both of whom had played quiet but meaningful roles in her life.

Nora and Agnes could hardly contain their excitement when the news reached them, and the dowager duchess, radiant with pride, declared that the late Duke of Ashford would have been *overjoyed* to see his son marry such a fine young woman.

Meanwhile, with Baron Brighton and Lord Dalton imprisoned and awaiting trial, long-buried truths continued to surface. The baroness, finally freed from the rooms in which she had been unjustly confined, was publicly declared of sound mind. The announcement came from Susannah herself, who was determined, at last, to right her 'father's' wrongs and restore what little dignity she could to her mother's name.

Elizabeth, who had been quietly serving in the household of one of Mariah's relatives since the Haywood ball, was sent for at Susannah's request. Mariah knew the reunion would be tense, but it had to happen.

When Elizabeth entered the drawing room, she froze. Her eyes flicked from Mariah to Susannah, her expression guarded.

"Miss Brighton," she said coolly, offering only the briefest curtsy before turning to Mariah. "Lady Mariah, my heartfelt congratulations. I am truly happy for you and His Grace. You both deserve every happiness."

"Thank you, Elizabeth," Mariah replied warmly. "Please, sit. There is something we must discuss."

Elizabeth hesitated before lowering herself into a chair. Her gaze shifted uneasily between the two women. Susannah took a deep breath.

"Elizabeth," she began, her tone unsteady but sincere, "I know you have every reason to despise me. I have treated you abominably for years, cruelly, unjustly, and nothing I say can undo that. But I swear to you, I didn't know. I didn't know that you and I are sisters until the night of Lady Mariah's kidnapping."

Elizabeth's brows drew together. "And how did you come to know?"

"It wasn't I who uncovered it," Susannah admitted. "It was Lady Mariah. She overheard Baron Brighton and Lord Dalton speaking of it. Later, she showed me the diaries, her grandfather's and Baron Brighton's mother's. They told the truth."

Elizabeth looked down, her jaw tightening.

"And you believed her?"

"Not at first," Susannah confessed. "But when I read the diaries myself, I could no longer deny it. Every word was true."

A heavy silence fell. Mariah glanced between them, then gently intervened.

"Elizabeth, when you learned the truth about your parentage... did you ever confront the baron or Gordon?"

Elizabeth nodded slowly. "I did. Both denied everything. Gordon told me he despised me, and I thought it was because I resembled my mother. I hoped he might one day see me differently, but he never did." Her voice trembled. "Even when Susannah struck me at the Haywood ball, he stood there watching from the stairs above the servants' quarters and said nothing. No reprimand. No comfort. Nothing."

Mariah's eyes widened. "He was there?"

"Yes," Elizabeth said bitterly. "And he did nothing. It was Mr. Swan and Lord Haywood who saw to my well-being afterward."

Susannah's eyes filled with tears.

"I'm so sorry, Elizabeth," she whispered. She reached across to take her sister's hand, but Elizabeth pulled it away, her expression unreadable. Mariah leaned forward gently.

"Elizabeth," she said softly, "no one expects you to forgive what cannot easily be forgotten. But Susannah truly did not know you were her sister. The baron used both of you as pawns, he fed your anger and your pain and used them to control you. None of what happened was your fault."

Elizabeth's eyes glistened, her composure faltering. Mariah continued, her voice calm but kind.

"Baroness Brighton has asked that both of you live with her, not as servants, but as her daughters. She wants to begin again."

For a long moment, Elizabeth said nothing. Then, slowly, she looked at Susannah. The other woman's expression was full of regret. Her hand still extended in silent plea. This time, Elizabeth hesitated only briefly before taking it.

Tears shimmered in both their eyes as their hands clasped, tentative, fragile, but sincere. Mariah smiled, her own eyes bright. Healing, she knew, would take time, but perhaps, at last, time was something they all had.

16

"God bless it – And Us"

Garrett and Mariah burst through the church doors hand in hand, laughter mingling with the joyful cheers of the crowd. Rice and rose petals flew through the crisp winter air, showering over them like tiny blessings of snow. The bells rang high and brightly above the churchyard, their sound echoing across the frosted hills.

Mariah's cheeks glowed with happiness as she paused to kiss and embrace her loved ones, her father, the dowager duchess, Nora and Agnes, and the many friends and relatives who had come to share their joy. Garrett, his arm protectively around her, guided her through the crowd to the waiting sleigh, its seats lined with thick wool blankets and a fur throw to keep her warm.

She turned once more before climbing in, her eyes sweeping over the familiar faces. Just a few months ago, she would never have imagined herself surrounded by so much love, family she hadn't known existed, friends who had become like sisters, and even those who had once been enemies now standing together in peace. Her heart brimmed with gratitude.

Near the church steps, she spotted Lord Winter and Baroness Brighton in animated conversation, their expressions softened and warm. The sight made her heart lift.

Perhaps they'll find happiness together, she thought with a smile. *Both deserve another chance at love.* And just beyond them, she noticed another unexpected scene, Lord Winter's brother, the reserved, silver-haired Baron Winter, speaking quietly with Susannah. The young woman's expression was gentle, her laughter genuine, and though he was nearly old enough to be her father, there was no mistaking the spark between them. Mariah's smile widened. *Even broken hearts,* she reflected, *can find healing.*

At a signal from Mr. Swan, the coachman clicked his tongue, and the horses leapt forward, sleigh bells jingling in rhythm with the steady clop of hooves on packed snow. The cheering faded behind them as Garrett drew Mariah closer to his side, wrapping his arm securely around her shoulders. The world seemed to soften, the whisper of wind through the trees, the golden glow of lanterns receding behind them, the clean scent of pine and winter air.

When Mariah looked up into her husband's eyes, she found them filled with warmth that made her pulse quicken. Her breath caught as he leaned closer, his lips brushing hers with fierce, unguarded affection. The kiss deepened, stealing her breath and leaving her trembling. The rush of the sleigh, the cold air, and the pounding of her heart blurred together into one dizzying, blissful moment. When Garrett finally drew back, his gaze lingered on her, tender and full of promise.

He lifted her chin gently, his thumb brushing her cheek.

"You have no idea," he murmured, "how long I've waited for this moment."

Her blush answered for her before she could speak. Warmth spread through her as she fought the urge to pull him close again.

His gentle touch sent a flutter through her, and she realized, with a quiet thrill, that now, as his wife, she no longer needed to guard her heart. Mariah met his gaze and saw the same restrained longing mirrored there. With a small, mischievous smile, she nestled against his chest, letting him wrap her safely in his embrace until the urgency softened into sweet anticipation.

Garrett chuckled softly and kissed the top of her head.

"We'll be home soon," he whispered.

The sleigh glided on until it finally came to a stop before the cozy little Christmas Cottage. Garrett jumped down first, his boots crunching in the snow, then turned and lifted Mariah carefully into his arms, as though she were made of spun glass. The footman unloaded their bags before turning the sleigh back toward Ashford, leaving the newlyweds wrapped in quiet, perfect solitude.

Mariah looked around the cottage and smiled in quiet awe. It was even more enchanting than she remembered, every garland draped just so, every candle trimmed and polished, every golden ribbon tied with thoughtful care. Evergreen boughs framed the mantel, their needles catching the firelight, while bowls of dried oranges and cloves lent the room a warm, festive glow.

The air was rich with the comforting scents of pine, cinnamon, and spice, wrapping around her like an embrace. It felt less like a house and more like a welcome, one prepared with affection and expectation. Someone, likely the dowager duchess, had seen to every detail, ensuring that the cottage shone in celebration of their arrival.

Mariah's chest tightened with emotion. This was no longer merely a place of refuge or memory it was the beginning of their life together. A home, however small or remote, made sacred by love, intention, and the promise of all the Christmases yet to come.

Garrett crossed to the hearth, stirring the embers with practiced ease. The flames sprang up at once, bright and eager, casting the cottage in a soft, golden glow. Mariah's heart gave a happy flutter as she watched him, the firelight catching in his dark hair, the relaxed confidence in his movements, the quiet, unmistakable joy written across his face.

When he turned and caught her watching him, his smile shifted into something wickedly tender. Without a word, he crossed the room in two long strides, swept her into his arms, and kissed her with breath-stealing passion. She melted against him instantly. Her hands braced against his chest as his lips claimed hers again and again. Laughter slipped between kisses as they both lost themselves in the simple, dizzying happiness of being together. At last he drew back, brushing his thumb gently across her lower lip, his eyes alight with mischief.

"I believe," he said playfully, "I still owe you a proper supper."

Mariah giggled, still breathless. "May I help you make it?"

He shook his head at once, entirely resolute. "Absolutely not."

Her brows lifted in mock offense.

"And why ever not?"

"Because, my love," he replied, leaning closer with a teasing smile, "your presence in that small kitchen would distract me far too much. I can barely think straight when you're near me now."

Her laughter filled the cottage, light and musical. Heat warmed her cheeks as he caught her hand and led her toward the sitting room.

"Sit here," he instructed, settling her gently onto the settee before the fire. "If you grow bored, there are books on the shelf. But no sneaking into the kitchen." He punctuated the command with a wink that earned another laugh before disappearing through the doorway.

For several quiet moments, Mariah simply sat there, her heart brimming. It hardly seemed real, she was married. Married to a man who had crossed a storm and faced death for her, who looked at her as though she were the greatest treasure he had ever found.

She rose at last and wandered to the bookcase, trailing her fingers over the worn leather spines before selecting a slim volume of poetry. Yet when she returned to the fire and opened it, the words refused to hold her attention. Every sound from the kitchen, the clink of a pan, the scrape of a knife, the faint hum of Garrett's voice, made her smile. Soon the cottage filled with the rich scent of roasting meat and warm bread, mingling with pine from the garlands and the gentle sweetness of wood smoke. The aroma wrapped around her like a promise, comforting and irresistible.

Smiling to herself, Mariah set the book aside and rose quietly from the settee. She followed the delicious trail toward the kitchen, her steps light, her heart overflowing with love and laughter, utterly certain that this, right here, was happiness.

Seeing Garrett standing before the stove, sleeves rolled to his elbows and a faint flush from the fire warming his handsome face, was a sight Mariah found altogether too appealing. For a long moment, she lingered in the doorway, simply watching him. There was something deeply captivating about seeing a duke, *her* duke, bent over a pot, utterly focused, his movements sure and practiced.

She stepped closer, her skirts whispering softly against the floorboards. Garrett turned as though he had sensed her presence before he heard her. The corners of his mouth curved upward in quiet amusement.

"I have to say, Your Grace," she teased lightly, tilting her head, "I never imagined your cooking would smell this wonderful. Perhaps it's only because I'm famished, but I cannot wait to taste it."

He raised a brow, his tone feigning offense.

"You think it's only because you're hungry? Are you implying I lack talent?"

She smiled sweetly, eyes dancing with mischief.

"Not at all. I am merely... surprised. A man who can prepare a meal that smells like heaven is a rather attractive sight."

Garrett's lips twitched into a slow, knowing grin.

"Is that so?" he murmured, stepping closer until she could feel the heat radiating from him. His gaze held hers, steady, unhurried, and entirely too intoxicating. Before she could summon a clever reply, he leaned down and kissed her, soft at first, then deeper, stealing her breath and leaving her pulse wildly unsteady. When he finally drew back, Mariah stood motionless, dazed, her lips parted in surprise.

Taking advantage of his momentary distraction, she quickly reached for one of the roasted vegetables cooling on the counter and slipped it behind her back just as he turned.

"What are you hiding there?" Garrett asked, his tone equal amusement and warning, one brow lifting in mock sternness.

"What makes you think I'm hiding anything?" she replied innocently, though her wide eyes betrayed her at once. He gave a low chuckle and stepped closer, his arm slipping around her waist with practiced ease.

"I would recommend confessing, my dear, before I'm forced to extract the truth... by rather persuasive means."

Mariah gasped as he drew her against him, his eyes alight with teasing warmth.

"You wouldn't dare?" she whispered breathlessly.

"Oh, wouldn't I?" he murmured, his voice a low rumble that sent a shiver down her spine. "Admit you were stealing from my supper, or I cannot guarantee I won't kiss you until you surrender."

Her heart fluttered wildly beneath her bodice. Slowly, she lifted her hand and returned the vegetable to its plate, her cheeks glowing pink.

"See? Nothing here."

Garrett's grin widened, pure mischief softened by unmistakable affection. He opened his mouth as though to scold her playfully, but she turned toward the stove, flustered.

"What are you making that smells so divine?" she asked, determined to steady her voice.

"Wild duck roasts," he replied, watching her from behind with fondness he did not bother to hide. "With asparagus and potatoes. And there are a few pastries my housekeeper sent this morning." His gaze softened further. "Will that do, My Lady?"

Mariah looked up at him, her eyes warm and shining.

"It's far more than I could have dreamed."

But as her gaze lingered, over his face, down the strong line of his throat, she noticed his cravat was gone, his shirt open, just enough to reveal a glimpse of tanned skin and the steady rise and fall of his chest. Her breath caught. Heat rushed to her cheeks, and when she looked up again, she realized he was watching her, his lips curving into a knowing smile.

Garrett closed the distance between them in two strides. He dipped his head and captured her mouth in a kiss that left her trembling. His stubble brushed her skin, warm and rough, and his scent, wood smoke, spice, and something unmistakably *him*, wrapped around her senses, unraveling every thought. His arms circled her waist, drawing her flush against him. Mariah's heart thundered, her fingers curling into the linen of his shirt as the world beyond the cottage quietly fell away. The fire, the snow, the food, everything dissolved until there was only him.

The kiss deepened, slowed, turned tender and breathless all at once. When he finally drew back to breathe, she caught the edge of his shirt and pulled him toward her again, unable to resist. That was all the encouragement he needed.

With a low, delighted laugh, Garrett swept her up into his arms. Mariah gasped, clinging to him as he carried her through the doorway, his lips never leaving hers. Each step was unhurried, deliberate, an unspoken promise woven into every movement. The warmth of the fire spilled into the next room as he crossed the threshold, the world narrowing to the steady rhythm of his heartbeat and the taste of his kiss, fierce, tender, and utterly consuming.

Mariah stood at the window, her breath fogging the cold glass as she gazed out into the soft cascade of snow. She drew her dressing gown tighter around her shoulders, though it did little to chase away the chill seeping through the panes. The world beyond the cottage lay blanketed in white, silent, pure, and utterly still. There was a serene beauty to it, yet a quiet ache tugged at her heart.

KISSED AT CHRISTMAS COTTAGE

It was the night before Christmas Eve, and the snow had fallen steadily for days, piling high against trees and fences, cutting them off from the rest of the world. Though the isolation made the cottage feel like a hidden sanctuary, it also reminded her that her father and grandmother would not be able to join them this year. She sighed softly, and in that moment, she felt the familiar warmth of strong arms encircle her. Garrett drew a thick blanket around her shoulders and gathered her gently against his chest.

"Are you all right, my love?" he asked, his voice low and tender, his breath brushing her ear. Mariah leaned into him, the tension in her shoulders easing.

"I'm fine," she murmured. "Just a little sad that I can't celebrate Christmas with Papa and Grandmama. I know they'll be all right, they're spending the holiday with Uncle Benjamin and his family, but..." Her voice trailed off as her gaze returned to the falling snow. "It still feels strange not to be with them, especially since this would have been our first Christmas together."

Garrett pressed a soft kiss to her temple.

"They'll be thinking of you," he said gently. "And your father will be happy knowing you are safe and loved."

She looked up at him then, her blue eyes reflecting the firelight. His expression held such warmth and steadiness that her heart swelled. He tilted her chin upward, and his lips met hers, slow, unhurried, a kiss meant to comfort more than ignite, though the familiar spark between them still lingered.

"Come," he whispered against her lips. "You're freezing. Let's sit by the fire." He guided her to the hearth, where the flames danced brightly, throwing golden light across the cottage walls. Garrett settled into one of the armchairs and tugged her gently onto his lap, wrapping both the blanket and his arms around her.

Mariah rested her head against his shoulder, her body gradually warming in his embrace. For a long while, they sat in peaceful silence, watching the fire crackle and pop, the scent of pinewood filling the air. At last, Garrett brushed a strand of hair from her cheek.

"You're quiet," he said softly. "What are you thinking about, my love?"

Mariah lifted her head and smiled faintly.

"I was remembering Christmases past. Lord Winter always used to read *A Christmas Carol* aloud to the viscountess and me. I could listen to him for hours. His voice carried such warmth." Her expression softened. "There's a line from that story that stayed with me. I memorized it so I would never forget the true meaning of Christmas."

Her voice grew reverent as she quoted, "'And therefore, Uncle, though it has never put a scrap of gold or silver in my pocket, I believe that Christmas has done me good and will do me good; and I say, God bless it!'" She turned her face toward the fire, her eyes glistening in its reflection.

"I think that's what Christmas truly means," she continued softly. "Not gifts or grandeur, but kindness, love, and remembering the greatest gift ever given to mankind."

Garrett's gaze softened as he listened. He touched her lips gently with his fingertips, his heart full.

"You're right," he murmured. "Christmas is about grace and giving, about love that expects nothing in return. My father believed much the same. He always said a good man measures his blessings by what he can share."

Mariah smiled up, at him, her eyes shining.

"Perhaps we could begin our own Christmas traditions next year, ones that honor both our fathers and the man who raised me."

His smile deepened, curiosity lighting his eyes.

"What sort of traditions?"

Her earlier melancholy vanished as she grew animated.

"We could prepare baskets of food and coins for families in need, and deliver them ourselves, so they know they're not forgotten. If we lead by example, perhaps other nobles will follow."

Garrett studied her with quiet admiration.

"You always think of others first," he said softly. "I couldn't be prouder to call you, my wife." He tilted her chin, his thumb brushing her jaw. "I love you, my darling. Mariah Haywood, you are my heart."

Her eyes filled as she smiled through the tears threatening to fall.

"And I love you, Garrett. Merry Christmas, my love."

He kissed her then, slowly at first, then more deeply, as though sealing her words between them. The firelight flickered across their faces while the snow outside continued its soft, endless hush. When they finally drew apart, Mariah rested her head against his shoulder, listening to the steady beat of his heart. The world felt still, wrapped in peace and warmth, and in that perfect quiet moment, she knew that no matter where the years might lead them, she would never again spend Christmas alone.

The End

Epilogue – One Year Later

Snowflakes drifted lazily from a pale winter sky, the town of Ashford hushed beneath its white blanket. Church bells chimed faintly in the distance, mingling with the laughter of children playing in the square. The Haywood carriage moved slowly down the lane, its lamps glowing through the flurries, the crest of the Duke and Duchess glinting gold beneath the frost.

Inside, Mariah sat beside Garrett, her gloved hand resting atop his. Between them lay a large wicker basket filled with bread, apples, sweetmeats, and tiny wrapped parcels, tokens of kindness they had prepared for those in need.

At each cottage, Garrett stepped down first, offering his hand to help Mariah alight. The townsfolk greeted them warmly, their gratitude shining brighter than any star. Mariah's heart swelled at the smiles and laughter that followed wherever they went. By the time the final basket was delivered, twilight had fallen, and the world glowed in soft shades of blue and silver.

When they returned home, the grand Christmas tree stood waiting in the drawing room, its candles flickering gently and the scent of pine filling the air. Mariah paused before it, watching the golden light dance over the ornaments. Garrett came up behind her, wrapping his arms around her waist and pressing a kiss to her cheek.

"Do you remember," she whispered with a smile, "how we decided a year ago that we would make our own Christmas traditions?"

He smiled, his voice low against her ear.

"And now we have. You've made this manor warmer than I ever imagined it could be."

Mariah turned in his arms, her heart thudding as she looked up at him.

"Garrett... there's something I've been meaning to tell you."

His brow furrowed gently, a flicker of concern crossing his eyes. "What is it, my love?"

She hesitated, her breath catching as she placed his hand softly over her stomach.

"Next Christmas," she said, her voice trembling with emotion, "we won't be celebrating alone."

For a heartbeat, silence stretched between them. Then Garrett's expression transformed, wonder and joy dawning all at once.

"Mariah..." His voice broke as he drew her closer, his hand trembling slightly where new life stirred. "Are you certain?"

She nodded, tears bright in her eyes. "Yes. I wanted to be sure before I told you."

A quiet laugh of pure happiness escaped him, half choked with emotion, as he lifted her off the floor and spun her gently, the snow beyond the windows shimmering in the fading light.

"My darling," he whispered, holding her close, "you've just given me the greatest gift I could ever receive." When he set her down, he cupped her face, his eyes glistening. "You've given me love, a home, and now a family. I swear I will spend every day of my life proving myself worthy of you."

Mariah smiled through her tears. "And I'll spend mine loving you."

He kissed her then, slowly, reverently, as the fire crackled nearby and the snow continued to fall. Outside, the bells of Ashford rang once more, proclaiming peace, joy, and promise. As they stood together before the glowing tree, Mariah rested her head against his chest, her heart full.

"God bless it," she whispered softly, recalling the words she had always cherished, "every day and everyone."

Garrett tightened his arms around her, his voice warm with quiet awe.

"And God bless our little one."

The candles flickered, the snow fell like lace upon the windowpanes, and within the walls of their home, love reigned brighter than the stars above. And on that blessed Christmas night, their hearts whispered the truest gift of all, love renewed, life beginning, and joy without end.

Did you love *Kissed at Christmas Cottage*? Then you should read *Duchess in Waiting*[1] by Rebecca Lange!

She was no lady and had no desire to be one...

Ellie was a whirlwind, a wild spirit, and it drove her mother mad. But Danielle Huntington had no interest in becoming a lady. She was in no rush to find a husband and would have waited even longer to be introduced to society, if it wasn't for her younger sister who insisted on having her older sister finally make her debut.

Despite her not wanting to go to London for her first season, Danielle falls head over heels for her childhood best friend, who is three years her senior. Although a baroness of the local ton and her

---

1. https://books2read.com/u/m2EQYd

2. https://books2read.com/u/m2EQYd

daughter constantly criticize and demeanor Danielle, she keeps her happy spirit.

Things change when she receives a letter from her beloved cousin, confirming Ellie's fears that Eleanor's husband mistreats and tortures her. Knowing, quite well, that a man coming to her cousin's rescue would put Eleanor in even more danger, Danielle is determined to get Eleanor freed and away from her demonic husband.

When her grandfather arrives, informing her that she is next in line to be duchess of the Huntington estate, Ellie refuses. But when her other cousin disappears during a visit to her sister, Danielle knows she has to make a deal with her grandfather and parents if she were to help, free and find her cousins.

Her mission is terrifying, but no amount of danger would stop her from rescuing her cousins, even if it meant giving up her own life.

About the Author

Rebecca Lange is a devoted romantic at heart. Though she has explored a variety of genres throughout her writing journey, her deepest passion lies in historical fiction—particularly stories set in the 1800s American West and the Regency era.

A passionate advocate, Rebecca uses her stories to raise awareness of abuse, human trafficking, and the devastating impact of drug and alcohol addiction. These themes are not woven in for suspense alone, but as a reminder that such struggles are tragically real—and that victims are never to blame.

She is also a firm believer in women's rights, inspired by the courageous women of the 1800s who fought to prove they were not the property of their husbands but their partners and equals. Rebecca upholds the conviction that violence has no place in relationships or marriage.

Originally from Germany, she was born and raised there before moving abroad in 2002 to serve a mission for her church in Scotland. A member of The Church of Jesus Christ of Latter-day Saints, she now lives in Utah with her husband, their two sons (ages 18 and 20), and two lively Yorkie puppies.

Her writing motto is: *Never Smut, Always Sizzling Kisses, Consistently Closed Door.* Rebecca delights in weaving passion and tenderness into her stories, offering what she calls "sweet and diet spice" romance. Diet spice—what is that, you ask? It's the thrill of longing gazes, passionate kisses, and close embraces that build anticipation without ever crossing into explicit territory. For her, the most powerful love stories are those that remain tasteful and teasing, proving that romance can be both heart-stirring and wholesome.

Read more at https://authorrebeccalange.wixsite.com/bookstolove.